"What are you doing?"

He ignored her frantic questioning. Instead, ne blocked out the sound of her voice and raised his arms into the air at his sides, his fingers splayed out as he extended his senses to scan the area. His power eased out, like extensions of his fingertips, stretching into the corners of the room, seeking, searching for the source of the magic he sensed.

It was here. Somewhere.

He had sensed it earlier on his arrival, but being that his aunt and siblings practiced magic on a regular basis he'd never given it a second thought.

This room, however, stank with it. He smelled the odor, something strangely like sulfur...

"A spell has been cast in this room," he muttered. A strange spell. Odd. A spell he'd never sensed before, something new. It felt off in some way he couldn't explain. Who would be working new magic of this kind in his home? And, in this room in particular. Aunt Petunia worked her spells in the privacy of her rooms upstairs, or sometimes in the gardens, but never in this room. And his siblings each practiced in their own private settings, places where they could concentrate without the threat of being disturbed.

He took a step closer to the center of the room where he sensed a surge of power. He shivered as coldness seeped into his skin. It wrapped around his arm, sinking into his flesh, right down to the bone.

The magic in his house was always full of warmth and gentleness. Goodness and love. This magic chilled him to the bone. His heart skipped a beat. There was fear, terror, pain.

This spell was full of darkness.

The Witch's Thief

by

Tricia Schneider

The Witch's Thief

Cover Art by *Debbie Taylor*

The Wild Rose Press, Inc.
PO Box 708
Adams Basin, NY 14410-0708
Visit us at www.thewildrosepress.com

Publishing History
First Black Rose Edition, 2013
Print ISBN 978-1-62830-078-9
Digital ISBN 978-1-62830-052-9

Published in the United States of America

Dedication

To my children.
For the laughter, smiles, wonder and happiness
you bring each day.
I love you with all of my heart!

Prologue

England 1814

"She's asking for you," Julia Grey said softly at the door to his laboratory. Drake Merriweather sat at his desk hunched over one of his spellbooks and continued his search for some manner of spell to cure his dying wife. Even Julia knew it was too late. Susanna had suffered enough from the disease that wracked her body with unendurable pain.

"It's here," he said, not looking up from the book. "I know it is."

Julia stepped into the room and flinched from the sulfuric smells of past failed experiments. Some still smoldered in a bowl on the table near the wall. For months Julia and her father had helped Drake and his wife with their crusade. While her father assisted Drake in his laboratory, casting spells of all kinds, Julia cared for Susanna, assisting her in the battle to survive each day. She fed her, clothed her, helped carry her to the window to gaze upon her garden.

"She doesn't have much longer," Julia said, resting her hand on Drake's shoulder. At her touch, he trembled. He crouched further over the ancient text of the book he gripped tightly in his hands, covering his face with the pages. Very slowly, Julia pried the spellbook from his fingers, placed it onto the table and closed the cover. At the sound of the book closing, Drake took a deep breath and straightened.

"Come with me. She needs you." Julia helped Drake stand, holding his arm for support as they walked out of the room. She guided him through the hall and up the stairs until they reached the door to his wife's chamber.

Drake paused. He stared at the door for several moments before taking Julia's hand away from his arm.

"Thank you for all that you've done," Drake said, squeezing her fingers. He looked at her, and Julia flinched at the pain in his eyes. It was something she had seen shadowed there before, but now that the moment had come, that he'd at last accepted there was no cure, no saving his beloved wife, she saw the last vestiges of hope wither and die. It faded slowly into oblivion. The only thing to remain was pain. A dark, depthless pain.

Julia's eyes filled as she watched him straighten. Another change came over him. He tilted his head up and took a deep breath. Then he opened the door and walked in.

Julia entered behind him. The sight of the woman, sunken within the sheets of the bed, her skin as pale as the snow falling outside the uncovered window took Julia's breath away. Every time she saw Susanna, the poor frail woman appeared worse. Now that the end was mere moments away, Julia could see the signs of strain on her face clearly. She appeared to have aged several decades in the single year since they discovered she suffered from Belit's Curse. Unlike a magical curse that could be cast by a practitioner of dark magic, Belit's Curse was an illness. It was a horrible wasting disease that took the magic and the life away from witches and sorcerers alike. It was said an ancient witch named Belit was the first to succumb to the disease. There was no known cure. Nothing could be done to dispel the pain that slowly crept into their limbs, crippling them until they could no longer walk or function. It did not stop until it ravaged their bodies, leaving naught but an empty, lifeless shell.

No one knew how the disease was transmitted, if it was transmitted at all. It seemed to only strike a few random unfortunates. In all of Julia's four and twenty years on this earth, Susanna was the only victim she had ever known.

"My love," Drake said, his voice strong and cheerful where moments ago Julia could barely hear him speak from his grief. "Miss Grey has said you have need of me. I am here, my love."

He sat on the bed beside her, taking one delicate pale hand into his. He smiled at her and his eyes reflected the love he felt deep in his heart.

"Drake," Susanna said, relief transforming her features, "at last..."

"I'm here, sweet." He brushed her dark hair away from her face. She leaned into his hand, tears streaming from her closed eyes.

"Oh, Drake, I do not want to die!"

The sound of the woman's pitiful cry broke Julia's heart. She grasped the doorframe, and squeezed her nails into the hard wood. She marveled at Drake's strength, at his ability to not be visibly crushed by his wife's pain and fear. He smiled, brushing her hair, and speaking softly into her ear. There were no tears from him, no moments of agonized anger at his helplessness.

In the last few months, she had seen Drake break down again and again in his laboratory, but he never showed any fear in the company of his wife. When in her presence, he was strong, confident, cheerful, unafraid of the possibility of losing her.

His confidence always lent strength to his wife, offered her hope and the will to go on even during those many days when she simply wanted to fall into a deep sleep and never wake.

"I do not want to leave you," Susanna cried out. "I want to love you. I want to have children. I have so much to do yet in this life!"

"Of course, my love, and you will," Drake murmured. "You will, I promise you. Did I not say that I would find the end to your suffering?"

Susanna nodded, her sunken eyes appearing huge in her sallow face.

Drake lifted his head to look for Julia's father. The gray-haired man stood in the corner of the room, his face ashen.

"Roger," Drake said, one hand waving for him to step forward. "Bring the potion."

Her father's head dropped. Julia saw he held a bottle in his hand, one she'd never before seen. He stepped forward, his steps slow and reluctant. When he reached the bedside, he hesitated.

"Are you certain?" Roger asked, his normally booming voice now a faint whisper. Julia leaned forward to hear. "If you do this...There will be no turning back. You cannot undo what will be done."

"I have no choice, my friend," Drake returned, a grim determination glinting in his dark blue eyes. He extended his hand.

Roger's hand trembled, his large fingers turned the bottle around and around.

Coming to a decision, Roger backed away, and took the potion out of Drake's reach. "No. I cannot allow you to do this."

Drake's face contorted with rage and shock. He released his wife's hand, grimacing when she cried out for him. He stood and walked toward Roger, who backed away.

"You will give it to me."

Julia's breath lodged in her throat. She stood frozen, uncertain what was being played out before her. What was in the bottle? Why was her father so reluctant to give it to Drake?

"I cannot let you," Roger repeated. There were tears on his cheeks.

"Drake! Do not leave me!" Susanna wailed, reaching out for him.

"Roger, I demand you give it to me. There will be consequences, I promise you!"

"It will damn you both! I'm saving your eternal soul, my friend, as well as hers."

"My soul will be in torment without her!" Drake growled as he advanced. "I can save her. I *will* save her. I vowed it. This is the only way I can achieve it."

"No!"

Drake lunged at Roger.

Susanna cried out, reaching for her husband. Julia raced across the room, well out of the way of the struggling men. She reached Susanna's side, grabbed her hands and blocked her view of the fight taking place.

"All is well," Julia said softly, crooning to her as if

she were a child. "A mere disagreement. All will be well."

Inside Julia raged. How dare they fight over a silly little bottle while this poor woman battled for each and every breath! But, she knew her father. He was a good, peaceful man. He would never act with violence if he did not have reason.

"Take me to the window, Julia," Susanna said, her voice raspy, her eyes wet with tears.

Julia nodded, then pulled back the blankets and helped the woman slide out of the massive four-poster bed. She took one arm around her neck and helped Susanna stumble a few feet to the seat by the window. Ever since she had weakened to the point where she could no longer walk, they each took turns carrying Susanna about. Drake would carry her to the laboratory where she would watch him work. Roger would carry her to the kitchens where she watched Cook create masterpieces out of their meals. But when her strength left her so frail that she could not leave her room any longer, Julia helped her to sit by her window every day, so she could look upon her garden below.

Susanna loved her garden. She had spent hours upon hours working her magic on the plants, helping them to grow for her spells.

The once beautiful and elegant garden appeared ashen. Even with a thin layer of snow covering what remained of her favorite spot, it was obvious to see the destruction cast upon it.

Drake had tested each plant, using them in his experiments and spells as he searched for a cure. He was certain it was a matter of time before he found the right combination that would stop the disease. But, the disease never treated each of its victims alike. One could suffer for ten or more years, while another might waste away within a few short months.

"So little time we have," Susanna said. She leaned her forehead and one hand against the glass. Her warm breath puffed onto the wintry glass. Drake and her father continued to struggle behind them, while Julia knelt beside Drake's wife, watching her eyelids blink wearily. "Do not let time escape you, Julia. You are blessed with it. Use it well."

"Yes," Julia said, holding Susanna's other hand.

Soon, the fogged glass of the window cleared.

Susanna's hand grew limp and lifeless. Julia rested her cheek against it as teardrops fell onto Susanna's skin.

"No!" Drake roared. He shoved Julia aside and took his wife into his arms. The potion successfully obtained in one hand, he uncorked the bottle and poured the contents into his wife's throat. "Drink, my love. Drink!"

The liquid splashed across Susanna's face and onto Drake's hand. He did not stop working it into her throat until the bottle was empty.

"All is well, my love," Drake said, tossing the bottle to the floor where it smashed. He lifted Susanna onto his lap and held her, gazing out of the window. "All will be well. I'll have you back again. I vow, my love. I'll have you back again."

Roger took Julia by her arm, helping her to stand. While she cried, Roger helped her from the room. She glanced at her father, his hair mussed, his lip bloodied, and his shirt slightly torn. He had fought well, but Drake was the younger, stronger witch.

7

"It's over now, Papa," Julia said, sniffling between her sobs.

"I fear not, my pet," Roger mumbled. He turned his face into her hair to place a kiss upon her head. "I fear it has only begun."

Chapter One

Bavaria 1817

Basil Merriweather crouched among the forested trees lining one side of Schloss Adler. It was a huge gothic creation built over a century ago. The tall arched windows gave it a menacing appearance. While he waited for Reed to return with news, he contemplated the wisdom of his decision. Was it wise to proceed as planned? Or was it lunacy?

Basil wished desperately to know the difference. He clutched the letter from Aunt Petunia in his hand. He'd reread it a dozen or more times in the last week, during which he'd traveled relentlessly to get back home. He trekked over the mountain passes of the Bavarian forest on foot where Reed had at last found him situated near a deserted peasant village. Then, as luck would have it, by horse and cart aided by the one trusting farmer they happened upon. But, it was taking much too long and Basil found he was unable to handle the rigors of travel as he once had. The quest was taking a toll on him, both body and spirit.

It was when they found the inn that Basil had decided to use the mirrors to return home. Reed argued, as a good assistant would, that it was too dangerous to use the mirror transportation in his condition. Any magic use at all was dangerous. But, Basil was resolved. He needed to get home. His family needed him. He'd let them down one time too many in the past and he refused to repeat yet another mistake, which caused his sisters to suffer more from his neglect.

Movement in the darkness caught his attention. He held his breath, awaiting the approach of the person who moved with stealth amongst the trees. It should be Reed, but he'd make no mistake by trusting his instincts now. It might not be Reed, after all.

His grip on the pistol tightened.

"Where are you?"

Reed. Basil heaved a sigh, relaxed his grip and lowered his weapon.

"Over here," Basil called in a loud whisper.

Branches spread apart and Basil saw Reed's face in the shadows of moonlight. Reed squatted beside Basil for a better view of the mansion.

"I've found your way home, Mr. Merriweather. The reports we heard in the village were correct," Reed said, smiling with accomplishment. He paused in his moment of glory when he looked closer at Basil. "How do you feel?"

The half-day's travel had been difficult. More than Basil should have attempted in his condition. He knew Reed was concerned, but he ignored the question to get to the matter at hand.

"Did you find a way in?"

Reed steadied his gaze on Basil's face. Basil knew his assistant saw too much. He saw the lines beneath Basil's tired eyes. He saw the way the pain had etched itself into his face. Instead of remarking upon it, Reed continued with the mission.

"Aye," he said. "There's a back entrance,

unlocked. Most of the servants are abed, the few who are awake still are in the east wing."

"And the mirrors? Do you know their location?"

"Second floor, near the front. A ballroom with one wall filled with them."

"Fancy, that," Basil remarked dryly.

"The Adler's enjoy their wealth. With so many to choose, you'll find the one you need," Reed added with a nod of agreement. "Are you ready?"

Basil nodded.

Reed's hand reached for his arm, and helped him to his feet. Basil brushed it off. Pride kept him from taking the proffered assistance. He leaned heavily against the tree for a moment before he followed Reed onto the dark path leading to the mansion.

Once inside, it was easy business to find the grand staircase leading to the second story. It took more maneuvering to find the appropriate room as they searched the upper floor. They moved quietly through the corridors, aware their movements might be discovered by the family currently in residence or the servants who worked there. Reed cast a spell to create a luminescent glow to light their path. The light floated like a miniature sun above his hand, or like a large candle flame without the candle. He also cast his magic to peer through the closed doors to see what was hidden inside. No need to risk being discovered.

Basil followed his assistant, his friend, feeling rather useless as he could not risk any more use of his own magic. Using the mirror for magic was going to sap enough of his strength to make it a danger.

Minutes seemed like hours until they at last discovered the ballroom.

Basil's eyes had grown accustomed to the dim, shadowy darkness of the corridors. As they entered the ballroom, he was assaulted by the brightness of Reed's light spell reflected in a dozen mirrors, all of various shapes and sizes lining one entire wall. Reed closed his outstretched hand, extinguishing the light. The nearly full moon shining in a cloudless night sky emitted enough light to see without the need for spells.

"Will one of these work?" Reed asked, his voice a hushed whisper.

Basil nodded. "I'm certain of it."

"Which?"

"A tall one," Basil answered. He reached his hand out to the one nearest him. It stood six feet in height and at least that much in width. He closed his eyes and concentrated on his power, stretching his magic into the mirror, seeking the correct destination. When he couldn't feel the connection he searched for, he moved onto another.

"I need one large enough to walk through," Basil commented, as he searched.

"There's plenty to choose from here," Reed said. "And if one of these don't work, I'll begin a search into the other rooms. There's bound to be more in one of the bedchambers."

"If one of these are not suitable to my needs, we leave this place. You have a wife and daughter to think of now. I'll not have you risk your neck any further, Reed."

"I'd not have wife nor daughter if it not for you, Basil. I'll do what needs doing."

Basil glanced at his friend to see the solemn look of promise pass over his face. He nodded his acceptance. He never need fear that Reed would abandon him.

He went back to work on the mirrors while Reed walked toward the windows to gaze out at the scenery beyond.

"The snow will make the journey difficult," Basil said, knowing the direction of his friend's thoughts. "You need not follow me."

Reed turned back to him. "I'll see you off first. Then I'll fetch Mary and the babe, and we'll be off to England as soon as can be. Do no worry on that. I'll bring your notes, correspondence and books. You'll want those to continue your work."

My work is finished.

Basil glanced at Reed before turning quickly back to the mirrors to hide the sorrow in his eyes.

But Reed saw the glance. A profound silence echoed throughout the room until Reed spoke.

"You will continue...won't you?"

Basil paused his search for the mirror. He lowered his arm, turning his hand over to watch the slight tremble of his fingertips. His hand fisted tight.

"I don't see the point, my friend."

"There's still time."

"Not much."

"Little, but enough. You cannot give up now."

A sound from the corridor silenced any further conversation between them.

They moved as one, walking stealthily toward the doorway to take positions on opposite sides. Reed lifted his hands in preparation. Basil heard the whispered prelude to a binding spell. Since Basil refrained from using his magic, he relied on his physical strength to subdue anyone who came upon them. If any broke free from Reed's spell, Basil was prepared.

They stood in silence, awaiting the men outside.

If they were caught and detained, there was no way Basil would live to get home in time. And he'd not let anyone stop him from getting back to his family, nor would he let anyone hurt his only friend. This was his last chance to go home, to make things right.

Two men. The voices in the corridor sounded friendly enough, amiable, relaxed, not the sound of men searching for intruders. One laughed at a crude joke the other told and soon they passed the door and the voices were gone.

Reed let out a relieved sigh before lowering his hands. "We'd best hurry, Mr. Merriweather," Reed said. Again they were master and servant, a role they had played for many years. "No telling when another insomniac will wander through."

They moved back to the mirrors where Basil continued his search for the proper mirror. He reached out, extending his senses like he'd extend a hand. It was similar to listening to a particular tune, only instead of hearing it, he'd feel it. He needed one that he could attune to the vibrations of a mirror in his home. If he could find the right vibration, the correct tune, he could cast the spell to connect the two and he'd be able to simply walk from this room to his room in England.

Just as he neared the end of the wall he stopped.

"This one," he said, wriggling his fingers to feel the vibrations of the mirror.

He found it. This was one he could match to the one in his house.

Reed grabbed the satchel Basil left by the door

when they had entered the room and carried it to him. He opened it and grabbed the bottle he had packed at the top for easier access.

He lifted the bottle to open it, but Basil placed his hand over it, stopping him. Reed's gaze lifted.

"Farewell, my friend," Basil said, disappointed with the lump that formed in the back of his throat.

Reed shook his head. "We will meet again."

"As you say." Basil smiled at his friend's optimism. He held his hand for Reed to shake, solidifying their good-byes. Reed took the proffered hand then pulled Basil into a brotherly embrace, slapping him solidly on the back.

"You will find it," Reed whispered in Basil's ear as he held him close. "Mary and I *will* see you in England."

Basil nodded to ease his friend's conscience. In his heart, he knew this was the last time he'd hear Reed's deep chuckle or see his boyish grin.

After they parted, Basil opened the bottle and shook some bluish powder onto the palm of his hand. He whispered some words and then blew the tiny particles into a cloud that clung to the glass of the mirror. He waited a moment, watching calmly as the solid surface of the mirror began to shift, to change. It wobbled and, in areas, the glass appeared to slide from one end to another. Shimmering waves crested, and Basil knew the portal was fully open.

He glanced at Reed with a nod, and then turned back to the mirror. Taking a deep breath, he stepped into the watery glass.

He slipped through easily enough. His arms and legs began to stretch, an invisible force tugged at him.

Even though it was uncomfortable and set his teeth on edge, it was not painful.

A moment later, he emerged on the other side, and stepped carefully into a darkened room. The flowery scent of lilacs hit his nostrils, like walking into a cloud of flowers. He inhaled deeply the aroma that reminded him of a woman from his past. Every lilac in the world smelled like her and he was just thankful that he came into contact with that particular flower as infrequently as possible.

Disorientation hit him in the total darkness. He flung out an arm, searching for a wall to lean upon until he could regain his balance. His leg hit an object and blindly his fingers fumbled against it. Recognizing the edge of a table, he leaned his weight on it, and prayed for the dizziness to pass quickly.

He knew that travel through the mirror would sap his already dwindling strength. But, he hadn't suspected this disorientation or the weakness that passed rapidly through his limbs. It had been several years since he attempted to pass through a mirror, but now he knew his condition was worse than he realized.

The table swayed, threatening to give way beneath his weight. He reached out a hand to search for the wall or something sturdy enough to hold him.

The darkness was impenetrable. He couldn't see a thing. Not even a hint of ambient light from any corner of the room.

Where was he?

He fought to control the hammering of his heart, knowing from past experience that the stress would only do him ill. But, this blindness was chilling. How could he know for certain that the mirror took him to the correct destination? If he had made a mistake, a minor error in calculation, he might have gone through another mirror, into another house.

And with the strength of his magic dwindling...

The limbs of the table succumbed to his added weight. He heard the crack seconds before his body followed. He crumpled to the floor. And though he tried to brace himself for the impact on the hard tiles beneath, his elbow smacked against the floor and light brightened the room.

At first, he felt relief that he could finally see, but a moment later he realized the stars that lit the room were a result of the pain from his head hitting the tiled floor. And then the darkness grew deeper...

****

Julia Grey's head jerked up, her finger poised upon a line from the ancient leather-bound text. She tilted her head, listening. Above the crackle of the fire in the hearth, she heard a noise unfamiliar from the otherwise silent library. Mrs. Prescott and her servants had retired for the evening over an hour ago, which was why Julia had crept downstairs to retrieve the hidden spellbook. With no one to witness her nocturnal reading, she had made herself comfortable at the desk with a candle for light and a fire for warmth.

Then another sound, this time a crash in the hall, sent her leaping to her feet. The chair fell back, echoing eerily in the sudden silence.

With her heart pounding rapidly from fright, Julia grabbed the candlestick and ventured across the room in search of the source of the unusual noise. It had come from the hall, she was certain, but who would be awake at such an hour? Whoever it may be, she'd need to form some excuse for her own presence. Hopefully, they'd take her word and return to bed. She'd need some time to return the book to its hidden niche without any prying eyes regarding her every movement.

When she opened the door, the light from the candle and the fireplace illuminated the hall, revealing a sight that made her blink in confusion.

A man lay on the floor, his face turned toward the wall. Had he fallen down the stairs? If so, he had taken quite a tumble since the foot of the stairs were several feet away. She saw the remnants of a hallway table scattered across the floor.

That explained the crash.

She took a step toward the man, thinking him a servant who had stumbled down the stairs in the dark, but stopped abruptly when she noticed the condition of his clothes. These were not the garments of a servant, nor anyone else who dwelled within Merriweather Manor this night. He wore a long coat and high black boots suited to that of a gentleman.

Julia surmised it could be Sage, stumbling in from a night of merrymaking as he was wont to do in the early hours after midnight. But, as the wind howled with snow, she took note that his boots were wet with mud, but his coat and hair appeared dry.

And his hair was light. Not at all like Sage's dark-as-night hair.

Clearly, this was a stranger come to call at Merriweather Manor.

Or an intruder.

Julia backed cautiously away, waiting for the man to jump to his feet at any moment. He remained unconscious on the floor, giving her the time she needed to fetch a poker from the fireplace. She returned to the hall, weapon in hand, prepared to do battle if necessary.

She leaned over him, peering closely to see his face. It was turned against the floor, giving her no way to determine his identity without rolling him over. She bit her lip with indecision. She should call for the servants. He could be dangerous.

He moaned.

What if she left to get help and returned to find an empty floor? If he roused himself, he could easily hide in any of these rooms on this floor to escape detection. Her imagination flew with possible dark scenarios.

No time to get help. She'd deal with this herself.

She took the poker, holding it in a threatening manner and advanced on him. Leaning over, she extended her hand to his shoulder and poked. He did not waken. She gave a little more effort and rolled him onto his back.

Now she had a better view with the illumination from the candle. It gave her just enough light to view him properly.

She looked at his face and knew she must be dreaming.

How else to explain the presence of this man?

Basil Merriweather.

Could this truly be Basil?

His blond hair fell over his brow in a careless wave. The features she had grown accustomed to as a child had morphed into those of a man. Stronger, masculine, and handsome. Surely, an artist created this face. She touched his cheek with one finger, just to be certain this was not some illusion. His skin felt warm and rough, a day's growth of golden whiskers bristled against her finger.

"Miss Grey!" Parker's voice echoed in the hall. She jumped, and snatched her hand away from Basil's cheek as if she had been burned. The poker leapt from her other hand so that she fumbled to get purchase on it. Grasping the metal rod, she held it against her chest, feeling the rapid beat of her heart and took a step back before turning to face Mrs. Prescott's butler rushing to meet her.

He arrived with shirttails bunched hastily around his waist and held a candle at arm's length in front of him.

"I heard a crash," Parker said on arrival, taking in the sight of the man and the broken table bits scattered around. "Is it an intruder, Miss Grey?"

"No, no," she said, shaking her head. A guilty flush crept up her neck as though she had been caught doing something improper, like caressing the cheek of a handsome, unconscious man. "It's Mr. Merriweather."

"Mr. Merriweather?"

"Yes, Mr. Basil Merriweather," Julia clarified. "Apparently, he has returned." She turned back to the man on the floor, wondering what had finally compelled him to return home after so long.

"By my word, it is Mr. Merriweather!" Parker said and knelt down to see for himself. "How did he come to be on the floor?"

"I don't know. Whatever mishap has occurred, he is in need of assistance. Would you help me bring him into the library? We can settle him by the fire. Then you must rouse Mrs. Prescott. We might have to send for the doctor."

"It's snowing fiercely now, Miss Grey," Parker said. "The doctor will have to wait until morning. It's not fit for beast nor man."

Blast! The blizzard. She'd forgotten. Being ensconced in the library for most of the night, the storm raging outside was the least of her worries. Just how did Basil manage to get into the house without a sound? Especially with wind that howled like a monster? It surely would have shook the doors when he opened them…

The corner of Julia's eye caught the sight of firelight from the hearth reflected in the full-length mirror hanging in the hall.

Of course. That explained it. He'd come through the mirror.

"Never mind the doctor, then," Julia said, kneeling down beside Parker. "Help me move him closer to the fire so we can ascertain his injuries."

"Very well."

Parker lifted Basil from under his arms while Julia gathered his legs. Together they hefted him carefully into the library. Thankfully, it was not a far distance. The man might not be huge of stomach, but he was tall and muscular, making his weight a great deal for a woman and elderly servant to carry. They managed to get him to the carpet by the fireplace where Parker lowered his charge.

"Are you all right?" Julia asked the butler, worried to see his face flushed red from exertion.

"Fine, fine," he muttered, catching his breath.

Julia took a moment to do the same. Then she peeled back Basil's coat, and looked for any signs of injury. Finding none, she took his head in her hands and searched for a wound that might be the cause for his unconsciousness. There was slight swelling at the back, which might explain why he did not wake. Other than that, she could see no obvious sign of any distress.

"Fetch Mrs. Prescott," Julia said at last. "She'll know what needs to be done."

"Of course, ma'am."

She watched Parker exit the room, wishing she could go in his stead. But she found it difficult to pull away from Basil. Her gaze wandered back to him. She knelt at his side, looking into his sleeping face.

"Is it really you?" she whispered in disbelief. Again, her hand wandered to his cheek, touching him there to be sure he was real. How many nights had she dreamed of him coming home? How many days had he invaded her thoughts? Now he was here and she didn't know what to think.

He'd been gone for so long. Ten years and two months to be exact. The last moment she'd seen him had been seared into her memory. He had met her in the garden that day. When he approached, she'd noticed the stiff set to his shoulders and something dark in his eyes she had never before seen. She had commented on it. He'd smiled, laughed at her worry and assured her all was well. Then he had kissed her. The sweetest, most memorable kiss of her existence. The next day, when she woke, she learned of his sudden departure. There had been no word from him until several days later when a letter was sent to Mrs. Prescott stating he had been called to London. A few weeks after, another letter stated his intentions to travel abroad.

He directed all of his correspondence to his aunt, never once mentioned Julia or inquired about her whereabouts. Any hopes Julia had entertained of a union between them were dashed within months when she came to realize that he was not returning home.

Until now...

Julia watched his eyes slowly open.

He blinked.

Then his gaze swept the room before fixing on her. Her heart leapt into her throat as his gaze settled on her, taking in her face, her clothes, her presence at his side. Her fingers tightened around her skirts, unwilling to move any other part of her body. Not able yet to believe her eyes, she dared not move nor make a sound for fear this image of Basil might vanish forever. Even Parker's presence tonight might be explained away as part of a bizarre dream.

Basil said nothing. He stared. She saw the puzzlement in his eyes. The way his brow crinkled slightly. After several moments, he carefully licked his lips.

"I'm dreaming." His voice was husky, rough from sleep. It sounded sweet to her ears. She smiled, surprised his thoughts ran the same path as her own.

"No," she said with a small shake of her head. She took a breath when she realized she'd been holding it while he silently observed her. She held her hands tight in her lap, yearning to reach out to touch him, but frightened by his response.

"Then I'm dead."

"Not at all."

"Julia?" he whispered. She bit her lip to keep from sobbing at the sound of his voice speaking her name in such a breathy whisper, almost reverently.

She nodded, hating the sensation of tears forming

beneath her eyelids.

"Where am I?"

"Merriweather Manor," she replied.

"Aunt Petunia?"

"Parker is bringing her down."

His head jerked up, and his gaze darted around once more as if only now noticing he lay prone on the floor. He made a move to sit up. Julia put her hands on his chest, gently pushing him back down. He struggled, but did not seem to have the necessary strength to push her away. He was weak, she realized. But, from what?

"Do not move," she said. "I found you unconscious in the hall. Mrs. Prescott will see to you."

"No," he said, and his eyes widened in sudden panic. "Help me up."

"I do not think it wise. It seems you are hurt in some way."

"Please," he said, and his fingers grasped her hand. Her breath left her lungs at the sensation of his warm hand wrapping around her delicate one. "Help me up. I cannot allow her to see me like this."

His gaze implored her. A shiver passed over her skin. The depth of his desperation sank into her, convincing her that she needed to allow him to retain his dignity. Being discovered prone on the floor by his elderly aunt would bring no one satisfaction.

"Here," Julia said and reached down to grasp his shoulder. "You must help me."

He struggled to stand with her there to steady him. Together they moved to the nearest chair, where he crumpled into the seat, clearly exhausted from his ordeal. She sank to the stool by his feet.

"What's happened? Are you injured?"

"No," he said, shaking his head.

Several deep breaths later, he looked down at her solemn face, studying her, tracing her each feature with his gaze. She saw some emotion there, something she could no longer identify.

He hesitated a moment, then asked, "Do you know me?"

Julia nodded, and fought the tears that threatened to surge beneath her eyelids. It occurred to her that although she knew this man's past, she did not know him now. He was a stranger to her. That knowledge hurt her, more than she ever thought possible.

"I know who you were," she answered. Her trembling voice sounded foreign to her ears. "Basil."

The corner of his mouth lifted into a small smile. He seemed about to say more when they both turned toward the sound of commotion coming from the stair. Julia heard Mrs. Prescott's high tones inquiring after Basil's condition. Parker would have told her how they found him.

"Do not mention the state of my health." Basil spoke quickly for they had only moments before his aunt arrived. "She is not to be made aware of your concerns. Promise me."

Julia swallowed hard, warring over her loyalty to his aunt who had come to care for her during her time of need and that of the man she had once given her heart and soul. The urgency in his eyes persuaded her. She nodded. He visibly relaxed.

What was wrong with him? What was he hiding?

She had no time for any further thought, for Mrs. Prescott bustled into the room, Parker at her elbow.

Tricia Schneider

Chapter Two

"Basil? My boy?" Aunt Petunia's voice pierced his heart.

He glanced at Julia. *Gods, it was Julia.* Dredging up every last bit of strength left in him, he forced his thoughts away from the woman beside him and stood on his own. His legs felt like pudding and his knee's trembled. He prayed he might remain on his feet until he could seat his aunt in the chair next to him. He did not want her aware of his condition. It had never been his intention to tell any of them. He'd not change that now.

"Auntie!"

"My stars! It is you!" Petunia's eyes widened, her smile blossomed on her rosy cheeks. She looked just as he remembered. Her hair was pulled under a cap, though several loose strands revealed the snow-white shade. Her blue eyes were round and wide and full of joy as she rushed with Parker's assistance to his side. Basil took a slow step toward her, trying to appear as though all was well. Several inches shorter than his own massive height, the top of her head barely reached his chest when she embraced him.

He smiled. How often in his past had he run to this woman in need of someone to soothe his hurts and ease his fears? She had been the rock he relied on after his parents' death. His caretaker, his strength. Now that he

26

was grown and their roles were all but reversed, he knew he'd need to appear as strong and confident as was possible. Especially if he wished to hide any secrets from her. Aunt Petunia was sharp as a blade. In his youth she'd seen through many of his childish lies. He only hoped that in her joy of seeing him returned, she didn't look too closely at what he didn't want her to witness.

"Parker tells me he discovered you unconscious in the hall," Petunia said, pulling away to look up at him.

"A mere trifling," Basil said. "When I stepped out of the mirror, I slipped and fell into a table in the hall." He lifted his hand to the sore spot on his head. "Like a fool, I hit my head."

"Basil!" she said, then motioned for him to sit in the chair. With immense relief, he obeyed. She took a moment to inspect his head, ascertaining for herself the extent of his injury. "A simple poultice will see this healed. I can prepare it momentarily."

"No need, Auntie. I'm fine," Basil said.

"Well, my stars, it does me good to see you, my boy!" Petunia stated then leaned back to get a good look at him. "You've grown. Why were you gone for so long? I could have been dead and buried before setting eyes on you again. Did I not say so, Julia? Many times over the years. Oh, Julia," Petunia said, turning to face the woman. "You know my nephew Basil. My dearly departed niece's son. You were much attached as children, if I recall. Basil, do you not remember our neighbor Miss Grey? It has been a long time, indeed, if you should forget her. She spent more time here with you than your sisters, to be sure! She's come to keep company with me at Merriweather as my lady's companion."

Basil made to stand, as a gentlemen should, but Julia stopped him. "No need for formal re-introductions," she said, smiling with genuine warmth. "We are old friends, are we not, Mr. Merriweather?"

"So old that we need not be so formal, I believe, Miss Grey."

A shade of pink lightly flushed her cheeks. She lowered her lashes, looking quickly to the floor, though her smile remained in place. "Indeed," she said.

Aunt Petunia began to chatter once more, marveling at Basil's physical changes and all the years that had passed since she last clapped eyes on him. Though he followed her dialogue, his aunt's voice fell to the background as Basil focused on the sight of Julia.

Julia!

Stray strands of dark brown hair curled softly against her cheek. The fire's light shone upon it, illuminating the reddish interwoven strands, a trait she shared with her younger sister. The color suited her pale skin and enhanced the jade of her eyes.

His nostrils twitched. Her scent of lilacs plagued him. Basil refrained from inhaling deeply of that beauteous odor.

The moment he opened his eyes to find himself on the library floor with her hovering over him, he had been convinced he woke to a dream. After all, he dreamt of her often. Even while he banished her from every waking thought, she still came to him at night, her hands searching for him, her heat warming him, her lips tasting him. He'd suffered many difficult nights with her memory tormenting him.

And to have her now, only an arm's length away

and unable to embrace her as he so desired tore at his fragile heart. He resisted for decorum's sake as well as her own good. He broke ties with her those many years ago. He'd not do her harm by engaging in her society now, no matter how much he yearned for her company.

Aunt Petunia spoke his name and he realized she'd ask him a question that he failed to answer while he busied himself with memories of Julia. He needed to pay better attention.

"Ah, yes. I came as quickly as I could after I received your letter." Basil rubbed his hands in front of the fire. He wondered if he'd ever feel warm again. "Where are the girls?"

"Lillian and Melora are with Uncle Arden."

"Whatever for?" Basil looked up abruptly.

Petunia's elder brother Arden Prescott rarely wanted much to do with any member of their family. Occasionally, he accepted Petunia as a guest in his home in Cornwall out of familial duty, but other than that he preferred the life of a recluse. He was obsessed with his alchemical work. Basil visited his estate as a child and recalled glimpses of a gray-haired man smelling of rotten eggs. "Why are the girls with Uncle Arden?"

"He's claimed guardianship over them," Petunia said, frowning. "He promised a Season, a chance for them to find husbands. I thought he was being charitable after all these years, so I urged them to accept. They've never been to London, after all."

"And?"

Petunia shook her head in remorse. "Lillian contacted me a few weeks ago. There was no Season. He's already picked men for them to marry. Sold them to the highest bidder, in fact. He's run out of money and found husbands in exchange for funds."

"The scoundrel!" Basil sat up. "He cannot force them to marry. Who does he think he is that he may coerce them?"

"His work has always been his obsession. I fear he's grown worse still since my last visit to Cornwall."

"I do not know why you insist on keeping contact with him. He's little more than a madman."

"He's my brother," she said, lifting her chin in defiance. "He's the only one I have left since your dear grandfather departed this earth. As children, Arden and I were the best of friends. I honor that memory despite what he has become. And, I believe people can change, Basil. Don't you?" Her left eyebrow rose inquisitively, daring him to answer.

He looked away. Yes, people could change. He changed much in the last ten years. In more ways than he cared to admit.

Basil glanced at Julia, whose gaze remained fixed on the fire, wondering in what ways she had changed, too. Her looks hadn't changed greatly. Julia's face remained much as the younger version he remembered, although her eyes differed. They looked older, serious. Her youthful exuberance had vanished. Things had happened to her, changed her, matured her in ways he was certain he didn't wish to know. Had he done that to her? The vibrant life he had seen in her eyes was now dulled with...pain?

He looked away from her. He'd go mad if he kept up this line of thought. Although he could blame himself for many things, he'd hoped Julia had managed to forget him as he promised to forget her.

And because he was used to the lies he told himself, his hungry gaze turned back to her, devouring the sight of her. He hadn't realized how much he'd missed her. The urge to reach for her, to take her and cradle her in his arms nearly overpowered him.

"Julia, my sweet, would you be a dear and run to my rooms to fetch my shawl? This vulgar snowstorm has the chill in this room going right through to my bones. We'll have Parker see to the fire. It's starting to die down," Petunia said.

Julia nodded. "Of course, ma'am." She obligingly stood, offered a brief curtsy and left the room. Basil couldn't help but note the look of relief in her face as she darted passed him toward the door. He resisted the urge to reach for her arm. He wanted nothing more than to gather her into his embrace so he could give her a proper kiss.

He still couldn't believe it.

Julia.

How was it he returned to find her living in his very home? Where was her husband? And the myriad of children he imagined she'd have by now? Although it pained him to think so, she should have her own household by now.

Aunt Petunia leaned over toward his chair, shaking him from his thoughts. She grasped his hand and squeezed tightly.

"I have missed you, my boy."

Basil smiled. His throat tightened at the tender emotion in Aunt Petunia's chubby face. He caressed her weathered hand, the affection he felt for his aunt warming him.

"I never imagined you would stay away for so

long."

"Nor did I."

"And with hardly a word? Basil, did they not have mirrors where you were?"

"In fact, Auntie, they did not." Basil released her hand and she sat comfortably back in her seat. "I've spent a goodly amount of time in wilderness virtually untouched by civilized man. Mirror communication was out of the question. I couldn't even post a letter. I hoped you wouldn't worry over much as I did promise to return."

"I assumed it would be a bit earlier than this."

Basil nodded, glancing to the door. How long did it take to retrieve an old woman's shawl? Turning back to his aunt, Basil tried to focus on her instead of the woman who had gone upstairs.

"And did you find what you were looking for?"

"No."

"Care to tell me the reason you hid away within the jungles?"

"I've explained in my few letters. I'm following Father's footsteps. Searching the world for special spells and practices to record in the grimoires."

"Your father's spellbooks might be the excuse for leaving England, but not *the* reason."

"That's the only reason, Auntie," Basil said. He turned back to face the fire and hoped his tired face did not reveal the lie. She was too perceptive by far. He prayed she'd not see the odd shudder course through him, nor the way his hand trembled on occasion. He clenched his fist when he felt one coming on, hoping to hide it from her. He wondered briefly how long he could manage to keep it all a secret. Especially with his foolish travels through the mirror. He knew better than to attempt it. Reed had tried to talk him out of it. But the urgency in his aunt's letters compelled him. It was not only his sisters that worried him.

"Where is Sage? Why has he not done anything to assist with Lillian and Melora's troubles?"

"Your brother's been delayed in London. As soon as the storm is done and the roads are passable, he'll join us here."

"Delayed?" Basil arched a brow.

Aunt Petunia gave him a knowing glance and shrugged. She knew his brother's habits better than he. Sage was a rogue or, as his aunt often referred to him, a free-spirit. He dallied with any woman with a pretty face and an embedded ring on her finger. Sage was not one to fall into a marriage-trap with a green girl. He much preferred a more experienced sort of woman.

Some things, it seemed, had not changed.

He glanced at the ceiling, as if he might see through the plaster and wood to the rooms above. Where was Julia? What took her so long? Having had a few moments to glimpse upon her only left him wanting more. He yearned to see her face again. He wanted to stare at her, to listen to her voice. He could be content to sit for hours and simply watch her. To be in the same room again. His skin ached to be near her.

Where was she? And, why was she here in Merriweather Manor? Was it simply as a lady's companion for his elderly aunt?

He sighed, lowered his gaze and turned his attention back to his aunt.

"You are the only one I could turn to, Basil. Sage will do all he can, of course, but he never held much sway with your uncle. Senna is visiting Hyacinth in Italy. They hope to arrive within the next month. And Drake, well... He remains secluded in his castle. Since Susanna's passing, he's much changed these days."

Basil nodded with impatience as his aunt catalogued his siblings and their goings on, but there was only one woman he wished to hear of and she was currently residing in one of the rooms above his head.

"Basil, you must put a stop to your uncle's horrid plans. You have been their guardian since your parent's death. You must do something to save your sisters from such unwanted marriages."

"As much as I wish to, I can do nothing at the moment. After the snowstorm moves on and the roads are passable, I will travel to Uncle Arden's estate and settle this matter." He leaned forward and patted his aunt's frail hand. "Worry not, Auntie. I'll bring the girls home."

She wrapped her other hand over his, squeezing tight. "Oh, Basil. I knew I could rely on you. You were always the one, you know. The most responsible."

"Auntie."

"No, it's true. After your poor parents were killed in that horrid carriage accident, you became parent to your siblings. You had no choice but to grow up quickly, to take charge of the family. To guide them, to help them grow into the adults they are today."

Basil smiled. "My dear Auntie, you discredit yourself. I relied on you to care for the children while I was gone."

Petunia shook her head, refusing the role of family savior. Basil knew, even if she didn't want to admit, he was no rescuer.

No, he was far worse.

A coward.

****

Julia hurried down the hall and ran up the stairs. She found the room given to her upon her arrival at Merriweather Manor over a year ago and closed the door firmly before she began pacing the floor. She wrung her hands. Her long skirts swept against the rug. The rhythmic swishing noise usually calmed her any other night. Tonight, however, it simply agitated her further. She scowled as her fingers fisted together.

"Whatever are you doing?" Marianne appeared at her side, conveying a look of annoyance at the disturbance Julia caused. Julia's sister slumped onto the winged back chair near the wall. She blew away the curls that fell into her face with a heavy sigh.

"We have a problem," Julia said, noticing her voice remained breathy and soft. She scowled further and cleared her throat. "Basil Merriweather has returned."

"What?" Marianne jerked forward, sitting straight. Her reddish curls bounced in the firelight.

Julia nodded. "He's newly arrived. He's downstairs in the library at this very moment. Oh, Marianne, I had not planned on this!"

"Calm yourself, dear. There's no need to go into a tizzy. So, he's home. Does he plan to stay?"

"He's been abroad for ten years or more. I'm certain he plans to remain long enough to renew his acquaintance with his aunt and the rest of his family. He has much to beg forgiveness for in that department after being gone for so long."

Marianne nodded and leaned back into the chair. She tapped her chin thoughtfully. "I wonder what prompted this return. Was he sent for?"

"Yes, Mrs. Prescott sent a letter," Julia said. "Something about his sisters and their uncle. I had a difficult time concentrating with him so near."

"You still have feelings for him?" Marianne asked in a rather shocked voice.

"None that I would admit to," Julia lied. Being eight years her junior, her sister had been very young, barely the age of nine, when Basil left. Julia was uncertain how much Marianne remembered about her relationship with the eldest Merriweather boy. She did not wish to prompt any more memories. "I was simply in shock. He's been gone over a decade."

"To be sure," Marianne muttered, and then waved her hand at Julia. "Oh, do please stop your pacing. My head is beginning to ache from it."

Julia stopped and stared. "Does that happen?"

Marianne scowled in annoyance. "A habit, I surmise."

"I do not believe I possess the strength to go through with our plans. Not with Bas—Mr. Merriweather in residence. There must be another way to find it."

"There is no other way. You have no choice, Julia."

Julia sighed. She clasped her hands and looked Heavenward as though for inspiration. She continued her pacing, even as Marianne frowned her disapproval. "It's one thing that I must lie to Mrs. Prescott, but I cannot lie to Mr. Merriweather. He will see through it. I know he will."

"He's been gone so long. Much has changed since then."

"True," Julia admitted. She stopped pacing to stare into the low flames of the fireplace. Much had changed. She had changed. From his reaction to her, it seemed he barely remembered her.

Had she meant so little to him? She squeezed her eyes shut, not wanting to admit to the pain burning in her chest. She shouldn't feel wounded. She'd done her best to cast him from her memories. It proved difficult for the first five or six years, until she admitted he'd never be back. Basil Merriweather had no intentions of returning. She'd hoped to forget him, and for a time she thought she had.

And, now he was back.

At a most inconvenient time, too.

Julia glanced at Marianne, who watched her warily. She noted the dark circles beneath her sister's eyes. Marianne was relying on Julia to finish what she set out to do. Julia couldn't let a little thing as Basil Merriweather stop her from finding that book.

Julia straightened and lifted her chin in resolution. Taking a deep breath, she said, "I can handle him."

Marianne's left eyebrow lifted in doubt, but being the supportive younger sibling, she nodded in agreement. "Of course you can. He does not know you anymore, does he? You're quite changed. You are not the same Julia Grey."

That was the truth in its entirety. She was not the same. She never would be. Too much had altered in life for her to ever go back. Instead, she looked forward to the possibilities of a new future for her and her sister. Any feelings she might have for Basil must be set aside. She refused to allow thoughts of him to interfere in her plans.

Taking another deep breath, she said, "I must go. Mrs. Prescott will be wanting her shawl."

Marianne stood to follow, but Julia stopped her.

"No, I'll be fine. You remain here. I'll let you know what occurs."

"I'll keep out of the way," Marianne said, a pout forming along her lower lip.

Julia shook her head. "It won't do. I need no distractions. None at all."

Her sister looked about to protest, but after a moment she relented. Sighing, she took a reluctant step back.

"Very well. But you must report back the minute you can. I don't wish to hide away up here forever."

Julia nodded as she left the room to find Mrs. Prescott's shawl and descend into the unknown.

Chapter Three

She knocked at the door, indicating her arrival. No need to walk in during a private conversation, as Mrs. Prescott was certain to have with her nephew as soon as she was able. Although Julia was privy to most everything that occurred within the Merriweather family, she still felt they needed their privacy. After Mrs. Prescott called to enter, Julia opened the door and walked into the fire lit room.

Her gaze immediately fell to Basil. Suddenly, she felt her breath shorten with anticipation. He was real. This wasn't a dream. Basil Merriweather was truly here.

Julia listened attentively to the conversation between aunt and nephew. She knew very well how Mrs. Prescott doted on Basil and loved him. The poor woman missed him dreadfully.

She wasn't the only one. Basil's sisters also adored him. His absence left a terrible hole in their family that none could fill, much like the hole in Julia's heart.

Julia tried not to think on that and instead focused on the fire, watching the flames dance rhythmically to a song none could hear. But, she wasn't strong enough to resist sparing a few secretive glances at the man in question.

Basil had changed much, in both appearance and character. His shoulders had filled out, broader than they were when she had seen him last. He looked more of a man now than the boy who left. His neatly trimmed hair appeared freshly cut. She yearned to run her fingers through the blond strands to see if they were as silky as she remembered. He possessed the body of a man well fit, not overly muscular, but a lean physical condition. He obviously kept active and was not prone to sitting in drawing rooms drinking brandy into the early hours of dawn. No, he appeared to keep physically active, keeping his body trim and fit and ready for action.

"Auntie, perhaps we could speak further tomorrow."

This drew Julia's attention back swiftly.

"It's late. I fear I'm fatigued from my journey."

Julia silently agreed. The circles beneath his eyes indicated a severe lack of sleep, despite his brief moments of unconsciousness upon his arrival. Comparing him to the image sustained in her memory, she could plainly see he looked older, tired, even exhausted from his world travels. But there was something more that she couldn't quite comprehend. He looked like a man weary from not only his journey, but from carrying the weight of the world on his shoulders.

What burden did he carry?

And what of those moments of weakness after waking on the library floor? He could barely sit up without her assistance. Had it only been from a blow to the head? He appeared perfectly capable of standing on his own after Mrs. Prescott entered the room. Julia had stood by his side, ready to catch him if he should fall. Although he seemed to waver for a second or two, he gave no other outward indication of any physical distress.

"Of course, dear boy. It is growing rather late, is it not? I suppose I should retire, as well." Mrs. Prescott stood and leaned on the cane Parker had fetched for her. The woman's knees popped loudly. Julia stood to lend an arm to her employer. Basil stood at the same instant, taking a step forward to lend his hand to his aunt. *Ever the gentleman*, Julia mused, noticing again that he stood without any assistance. It must have simply been the knock to his head that had done him in earlier.

Mrs. Prescott waved him away and leaned on Julia's arm instead.

"Julia will see to me, Basil. And, I will see you at breakfast."

Basil grimaced. "Could I beg one day to sleep? I could use the rest, Auntie. You've no idea how long I traveled."

Again, Julia saw that weight hanging over him, dragging on his shoulders.

Mrs. Prescott clucked her tongue. "You have much to do tomorrow. No time for sleeping the day away."

She was surprised by Mrs. Prescott's response. Surely the old woman noticed his exhausted state?

"Yes, Auntie, of course," he said, the grimace remaining in place. Basil leaned over and kissed the old woman's forehead. "Good-night, dear. Sleep well."

Mrs. Prescott smiled. When he stepped back, his aunt continued to stare at him, tears shimmering in her eyes. With a contented sigh, she said, "It's so good to have you home, Basil. So good."

After that, Julia assisted the old woman, letting her lean on her arm as they departed the room.

****

She returned moments later.

"Pardon," Julia said, striding with caution into the room, doing her utmost not to look at him directly.

A mixture of amusement and desire flamed through Basil's blood. He refused to move aside as she reached for Aunt Petunia's shawl, her body mere inches away from him. He closed his eyes for a brief moment, remembering the heat of her skin.

When she made to back away to escape the way she'd come, Basil grabbed her upper arm, his fingers sliding around her with gentle firmness.

"What are you doing here?"

She faced him, looking up at his towering height, her eyes as wide as saucers. "I'm returning for Mrs. Prescott's shawl. No one noticed it slipped from her shoulders when she left."

His grip on her arm tightened.

"That's not what I meant. What are you doing in Merriweather Manor?"

"Oh," she said, yanking her arm from his grip. "Care to explain why you left with no word?" The venom that slid off her tongue was not something he remembered from the Julia he had known. This was new.

What could he say? How could he apologize for his cowardice?

"I don't know what came over me. I should have told you. I apologize."

Julia shrugged, tilting her head high with annoyance. She lifted the shawl and folded it over her arm.

"Good," she said, then left the room.

Basil watched her leave. He opened his mouth to call out to her, to beg her to come back, to talk with him. He had so many questions.

Instead, he let her go.

****

An hour later, Julia held the candle high as she maneuvered back down the stairs, keeping one hand on the banister for support. She tread lightly, tip-toeing where she knew she needed, since the stairs were old and creaked in certain places. Once she descended onto the first floor, careful steps led her back to the library.

The door was open.

She poked her head into the room, noticing the fire still alight in the fireplace. Odd that Parker hadn't seen to the fire. A quick survey of the room confirmed she was alone. She walked to the desk where she had placed the book she'd been reading earlier in the evening, just before Basil Merriweather crashed back into her life. The book lay in the exact spot she'd left it.

She set the candle down and nudged the chair closer as she sat. Opening the book, she left it thud softly onto the desktop. After flipping with gentle care through a few of the pages, she found where she had left off and resumed her reading by candlelight.

Until a man cleared his throat.

Julia's head shot up, and her mouth turned into the shape of a little "O."

Basil Merriweather sat in one of the winged backed chairs facing away from the door. She hadn't seen him when she entered the room. He nestled in the chair with a blanket wrapped around his shoulders. The circles under his eyes appeared more pronounced in the firelight.

"Miss Grey," he said with a nonchalant nod in her direction. As if this was an everyday occurrence that he should meet her in the library after midnight. She stood in one quick motion, bumping the desk with her knee and nearly knocked the candle from its perch. She lunged to grasp it, to keep it from falling. In doing so, it sputtered and died. A tiny wisp of smoke curled into the air. Through it, Basil watched her.

"Care to explain?"

"Certainly not." She tilted her chin defiantly. She refused to allow him to unsettle her nerves. Not again. After snapping the book closed, she made to march from the room, head held high.

"Please, don't," he said. "Don't leave. Not yet."

Her feet froze. Her heart lurched.

Never had she heard Basil sound so desperate, so...weak. She peered through the semi-darkness, trying to discern the reason for such a thready voice. Seeing none from here, she stepped toward him, curious.

"Sit." He nodded to the chair in which Mrs. Prescott sat earlier. It was close to his. She bit her bottom lip, weighing with heavy judgment whether she should sit beside him or across from him.

And then she looked at him again. She didn't like what she saw. Though it was difficult to tell for certain in the firelight, the pallor of his skin seemed extraordinarily pale. Dark shadows smudged across the underside of his eyes. Even his cheeks looked hollowed, probably from the shadows the flames chased across the room.

"Are you unwell, Mr. Merriweather?"

"Please, Julia. We once were well enough acquainted to forgo the use of proper names. Will you not call me Basil again?"

She sat gingerly on the seat beside him and folded her hands primly in her lap. She tilted her head and looked into his face.

"That was a long time ago…Basil."

At the sound of his name, he smiled. The smile relaxed the lines on his face, making her realize how tense he was moments ago. She peered at him closely.

"What's happened to you?"

"The very question I wish to put to you," he said. She narrowed her eyes, knowing he evaded her question by tossing it back. She pressed her lips together, determined not to answer any of his questions. *Let his curiosity fester*, she decided.

"I admit I'm quite surprised to find you here. I thought you married with six or seven brats by now."

"How do you know I'm not widowed?" she asked simply to torment him. Let him imagine her life being full of love and laughter while he was away. A delicious moment of retribution. She still felt the pain of his departure deep in her heart. "I could have ten children by now for all you know or care. My life may be blessed with fruitfulness and prosperity."

He stared a full moment, studying her. Did images of her possible husband flit through his mind? Did he wonder whom she might have married?

She wanted to torment him. He hurt her cruelly when he disappeared all those years ago. And with no communication after his departure, she only knew of his whereabouts from the gossipmongers in town. Even his family knew very little about the where's and why's. After all of these years, wondering and worrying over him, he returns with nary a word of explanation. Not a word about anything! Why did he leave? Where did he go? Why did it take so long for him to return? Had *he* married?

That last question had plagued her for more years than she cared to admit. Even now it sent daggers of pain into her heart. So, let him believe she lived a perfect life. Better than him knowing the truth.

"He died?"

"What?" Julia blinked. How did he know? Did someone write to him, explaining her misfortune in a letter? She didn't think anyone in his family took much notice of her after she relocated to London. She rarely traveled in the same circles as his brother and sister who lived there. She could barely count the times she might have seen them in the last five years. So, how did Basil know?

"Your husband. He's dead?"

Oh.

Her imaginary husband. Well, yes, he was truly dead and gone. When Julia was a girl she hoped Basil would one day ask for her hand. Those dreams died when he left England to roam across the world. Now that he sat in front of her, inquiring after her deceased imaginary husband, she guessed she might as well admit to the sad truth. As much as she wished to torment him, he'd find out the truth from his aunt if she lied.

"I never married."

"You never…?" This time Basil blinked. It took a moment for the information to sink into his brain. Then he struggled against the blanket like it turned into a heavy iron manacle designed to imprison him. He leaned forward, his eyes wide and wild. Julia inhaled sharply at the sight. For a moment, he looked like a madman.

"What happened to Walters? Were you not to marry Walters?"

Julia stared incredulously. "Walters?"

"George Walters."

The mere notion of marrying George Walters made her laugh. True, at one time they were friends. They spent many days at George's home at Bramford. As children, the three often roamed the forests outside of Meryton, the village near Merriweather Manor.

But, all that changed after Basil left. George's interest in their friendship waned. He moved to London. Julia stayed home, caring for her father and young sister.

"Why ever would you imagine I married *him*?"

Basil stilled. Then in jerky movements, he leaned back into the chair, gathering the blanket back over his arms.

"I... Someone must have written the news in a letter. I was certain you married long ago. Shortly after I left, in fact."

"Well, you were misinformed," Julia said. "He never asked me to marry, and even if he had I would have said no."

Basil stared in solemn silence.

Julia narrowed her eyes. She wished she had the power to peek inside his mind. What was he thinking? Why had he thought she'd married George Walters, of all people? Did he not know her feelings? Had she not made it plain to him when they were children? Or after they had grown? Just before he left?

She remembered the kiss they shared beneath the willow tree outside their village. Surely, he had known her heart's desire. She must have spoken of her love for him. Before she knew it, he was gone, off to roam the world to seek his fortune, or some such. No one knew quite why he left so suddenly.

But, Julia knew.

It only made sense.

He left because of her. She, the silly girl, who had declared her love. And he fled. She remembered the day vividly. After spending most of their childhood together as friends, sharing grief over the death of his parents, watching each other grow from children into adults, Julia at last shared her desire for him one spring day ten years ago. Quick as a flash, he disappeared. Like magic. Her lips twisted in a sardonic smile. Basil was good at magic. She wished he'd cast a memory spell over her before he left, something to make her forget the pain.

"Julia."

She stood and shook her head.

"It's late, Basil. Too late to discuss any of this." She moved around the chair, placing it between them like a shield. "Do you need anything before I leave? A drink? Something to eat? You look rather pale, I believe."

"N-no," Basil said. Then more firmly, "No. I'm quite all right."

"You do not look it."

The corner of his mouth curved into a wry smile. "I appreciate the observation, but I assure you, I'm fine."

Julia nodded. She cast one more inquiring look in his direction. She thought of the book, but decided it was best not to draw attention to it. She'd come back for it later.

"Good night," she said and left.

****

Basil wasn't all right. He shivered and tugged the blanket closer to his chilled body. The heat from the fire did nothing to warm him. He wished more than anything to crawl to his room, find his bed and get some much needed rest, but he feared he wouldn't make it to the stairs without collapsing.

Ringing for the servants to assist him was out of the question. They would run to Aunt Petunia in the morning to share this bit of news about her nephew's failing health. News he did not wish for her to know. In fact, he didn't wish for anyone to know. Bad enough his brother guessed the truth years ago. No one else needed to know his fate.

Basil shook his head in disgust.

After all of these years of subterfuge, of keeping secrets, he goes and asks Julia Grey to stay and talk with him, knowing full well she was an intelligent woman and able to see through his lies. It was one of the reasons he never said good-bye to her when he left. It nearly killed him to leave like that, but she would have seen the truth if he hadn't.

The truth he wanted to keep hidden.

Or did he?

He admitted his brother's knowledge of his condition brought him some relief. When his time came, at least one member of the family would know the reasons why. That he didn't hurt the people he loved because of recklessness, frivolousness, or vanity.

No, he tried to protect them.

Then why ask Julia to stay? While Basil shivered beneath this blanket, he asked her to sit in the chair across from him. She was bound to see something was not quite right.

And she had.

After all, she witnessed his disorientation upon his arrival.

She knew something was wrong. She just didn't know what.

Basil sighed. He wished his brother was here now. Or Reed. Reed would have talked sense into him. He would have sent Julia back to her room straight away.

Then Reed would have helped him to his room when the signs of the attack first reared their dismal head instead of gazing into the fire, thinking about her.

Julia.

His memory did her no justice. Either she was more beautiful than he remembered, or she had grown as such. Thoughts and memories swirled together while he gazed into the flames. They had grown up together. Being neighbors and friends with each other's families made it easy to spend time together. While at first she was content to play dolls with his sister, she soon found her way outside to practice sword-fighting with him and his brothers. George Walters was another of their group. Another neighbor, though his family wasn't so closely connected as hers. But, they were the best of friends. And as the years grew so did they, until he began noticing the changes between them. She slowly grew from a girl into a woman, he grew from a boy to a man. Their feelings for each other deepened, entwined like the thickest of vines. It felt right they be together. They'd always been together.

And then he remembered the kiss. The one and only kiss they shared beneath the willow tree outside of

Meryton. So deep was he trapped in nostalgia that he hadn't felt his hands begin to twitch. He didn't feel the cold run through his veins or the sweat break out upon his brow. It was not until his knees began to tremble that he noted his weakened strength.

He had thought to sit, simply to catch his breath until he could gather the last remnants of strength to drag himself off to bed.

Basil cursed himself.

The journey to Merriweather Manor had been arduous. After receiving Aunt Petunia's desperate summons, he departed for England immediately, intent to rush to his sisters' rescue. During the trip he did not rest as he should, and then he used his magic for the mirror.

Fool!

Now he must face the consequences of his actions.

He should have gone straight to bed after Aunt Petunia retired. Instead, he lingered by the fire, daydreaming of Julia.

He found the blanket Aunt Petunia must use to keep away the chill from old bones nestled next to her chair. He pulled it, covering himself as the shivers increased. Basil resigned himself to spend a sleepless night on the chair when Julia walked in.

He assumed at the time she needed a good book to help her fall asleep. Dare he think he was the cause for her restlessness?

No! He couldn't think that! She was supposed to be another man's wife. But she wasn't!

That fool Walters!

The spell should have worked. Had he done something wrong? Not used enough of some ingredient? It should have worked. Love spells had never been his *forte*. He must have mixed something incorrectly.

Basil sighed and shivered.

Who was he fooling? Nothing seemed to work. Especially in recent months.

He cursed. Loudly.

All these years he thought she married Walters. Married and protected. Cared for. Safe. Safe from Basil. With Julia married, Basil had no reason to return. In fact, her being married acted as incentive to stay away.

He feared if he returned, he'd regret all he'd done to keep her safe. He didn't want to see her on the arm of that fool. He couldn't bear the sight of them together, holding hands, kissing.

Basil growled.

But, she wasn't married!

What had become of her in the last ten years? How had she ended up in Merriweather Manor, as Aunt Petunia's companion? Practically a servant?

And what was she doing coming to the library, disrupting his restless slumber, looking for that damned book?

He glanced over at the desk where she left it.

It was a thick volume. From this distance, he couldn't see the contents or any details on the leather bound cover. He leaned forward, curious as to what type of reading she preferred. As he looked closer at the tome, a chill trickled down his spine.

It looked like…

But, it couldn't be…

Basil grasped the arm of the chair and struggled to his feet. He swayed then tightened the blanket around his shoulders. On wobbly feet, he shuffled toward the desk, wondering vaguely if he'd have the strength to return to the chair.

But, he needed to see this book.

He had to reassure himself it wasn't what he suspected.

When he reached the desk, the coldness that ran through his veins wasn't from the condition of his health. His fingertips lightly brushed the leather encasing the volume. He traced the letters carved into the cover. Opening the front cover, he peered at the pages.

His father's spellbook.

One of them, at any rate. But, Basil had hidden them, safe from prying eyes. Only Aunt Petunia knew where they were hidden.

He lifted his head and found the space above the mantel, with the flap for the secret compartment. It was closed.

She'd closed it after retrieving the book.

But, why leave it here, out in the open? Did she not know of its contents? Of the power it contained?

Or the evil?

His vision wavered. He gasped and tightened his hold on the edge of the desk. Hot and cold coursed through his veins. Sweat beaded on his brow.

Glancing at the chair, calculating the distance, he knew he wouldn't make it in time. After suffering from this damn condition for ten long years, he knew full well the signs.

He managed to drop to his knees with relative grace before the darkness closed in.

Chapter Four

What was taking him so long?

Julia's feet itched to pace, but she feared the noise might wake someone. She tightened her fingers on the banister as she crept for the third time this night down the stairs until she arrived at the library.

The fire was still lit, but the chair was now empty.

Basil was gone.

Strange.

After Julia left him in the library, she'd hurried up the stairs, but lingered, waiting for him to depart. With the sight of exhaustion she'd seen on his face, he'd get himself to bed soon. After all, he'd had a long and surely exhaustive journey. It explained the shadows beneath his eyes, and the tightness around his lips.

Although she waited, and waited, and waited more, he did not appear.

Perhaps he'd fallen asleep in the chair?

How uncomfortable. Also deserving. What did she care if he woke with a crick in his neck and a pain in his back? After the long years of heartsickness she suffered?

Julia chastised herself. It had been so long ago. And though she loved him dearly, she had said her good-byes to him, even if they were only whispered to the wind.

If he had fallen asleep in the chair, she should wake

him. Urge him to find his slumber abed. She hesitated, not sure if he might find her reappearance in the library suspicious.

But if she left him there, how would she manage to retrieve the book without his knowing? Unless he was in a deep sleep. Perhaps he would not hear her?

That's why she decided to creep down the stairs, yet again, to survey the room for possibilities.

But she saw no sign of him. Even the blanket Mrs. Prescott sometimes wore over her legs, the same she had seen him using, was gone.

How odd. She'd kept a close and attentive eye on that door. Perhaps she had blinked, and he'd already left. He must have moved fast. Or had he used magic?

Julia narrowed her eyes. Leave it to Basil to use a spell to transport him to his room. What a wasteful use of spell power.

At any rate, he was gone. Julia could now safely get the book from the desk and take it to her room where no one would see her reading. Searching. She needed one spell, after all. Not the entire book.

She moved with quiet steps toward the desk, staring at the book.

It was opened.

She gasped. She was certain she'd closed it. She looked around the room, peering into the dark corners, waiting for Basil to jump out with accusations.

She should have never let the book remain. But, it was too conspicuous to take the book while he watched. Surely, he'd ask what she was reading. He'd recognize it. And how could she lie? Even as children, he'd seen through her lies.

Julia hurried to the desk, grabbed the book and

closed the cover, glancing around again to see if anyone watched her.

No one.

Lifting the book and clasping it in her arms, she took a step and felt something against her foot. Peering down, she saw a boot.

She froze. She had difficulty comprehending what she saw.

A boot? Who left a boot on the library floor?

Leaning forward to peer behind the desk, she saw the boot attached to a leg. A leg she recognized.

"Basil!"

She dropped the book back on the desk, ignoring the loud thud that echoed through the room. Falling to her knees beside the inert body of Basil Merriweather, she feared he was dead. He hardly seemed to be breathing until she touched the skin of his cheek.

Julia snatched her hand away from him. Like touching fire.

He was feverish.

"Basil?" Julia tried to wake him by brushing a few strands of the cropped hair at the top of his head. The golden strands were soft and silky, just as she remembered. Her fingers drifted onto his cheek. The tiny hairs of a day-old beard prickled against her skin.

She patted his cheek, tenderly, trying to rouse him. When that failed to work, she struck a little harder.

Still nothing.

Julia leaned back on her haunches, clasping her arms around her knees and looked around the room.

What should she do?

Worrying her bottom lip, she considered calling the servants to assist. Surely a few of them could carry him up to his room. A quick glance at the large body lying on the floor made her adjust her estimations. A few might not work. He was finely muscled. And tall. They might need to wake the neighbors to ask to loan their servants, too.

Such nonsense! Julia shook her head from her musings. Seriously, her gaze should not keep wandering over his body in delicious appreciation. The poor man was ill, yet she ogled him as if she'd never seen a slumbering man.

She cocked her head to the side.

Well, she never had seen a slumbering man. Other than her father, but that wasn't like this.

Basil was most definitely *not* like her father.

Her gaze once again swept over him, taking in his handsome features and traveling down his torso. Did he have difficulty breathing? Perhaps the cravat tied round his neck was a bit too tight. She loosened it a bit, opened a button or two of his shirt, exposing his chest. Yes, he just needed more air. Maybe a few more buttons should be loosened?

Heat flooded her cheeks. What was she thinking? He breathed through his nostrils not his chest. As much as she desired to see his chest, now was not the time to give in to such curiosities.

She forced her gaze away from Basil and tried to focus on the situation.

He was ill.

That was plain to see.

He must have known he was ill and had not mentioned it to anyone. That was why he did not wish for her to say anything about his weakness earlier. He did not wish his aunt to worry.

His aunt!

Julia's head jerked up. That's it!

She jumped and nearly knocked into the desk as she lost her balance scurrying over Basil's body. She hurried to Mrs. Prescott's chair where, lying on the table beside it, sat her smelling salts. Mrs. Prescott always kept them near, especially in need for when she read letters from her brother. The man was always writing such astounding things to his sister, causing her upset.

Julia grabbed the smelling salts and rushed back to Basil, falling to her knees. With one hand, she lifted Basil's head and waved the bottle beneath his nose.

It took two passes before his nose crinkled, and his eyelids flickered. She put the bottle down and held his head on her lap as he came awake. His gaze met hers.

She smiled.

****

"What am I doing on the floor?"

"Again? I was about to ask you," Julia said. He made no motion to rise. Just rested his head on her lap and stared at her face. She took the liberty of returning her hand to his hair. She brushed a few tendrils, running her fingers again through the silky strands. It felt so soft.

"What are you doing?"

"Helping you."

"With my hair?"

"It's in need of brushing." That comment won a smile.

"Of course," he said with a wry quirk to his lips. "Whenever I wake mysteriously on the floor of the library, my hair is in desperate need of brushing. Lucky you were here to save my appearance."

"I am so glad to be of assistance," she said, smiling back. But, her smile faded as a tremble shuddered through him. And then another. His body was shivering, shaking. It appeared he had no control over it.

"Basil, what's wrong? What's happening to you? Are you ill?"

At the sight of her frown, Basil's amused smile vanished. He sighed, closing his eyes.

"Will you help me to my feet?"

He struggled to sit upright, while she kept an arm on his back, guiding him. He clasped the edge of the desk and used it to push up. Julia took one arm, not so much lifting, but helping to keep him steady.

As soon as he stood on his feet, he looked in worse shape than she imagined. He swayed. His knuckles turned white as he grasped the desk's edge. She kept her arm clasped around his, knowing if he lost consciousness the best she could do was guide his descent.

He was a very big man.

"Basil, this will not do. I must call Parker for some assistance."

"Parker? And what will he do? The man is older than the Bible. He can't help me."

"Then let me fetch Mrs. Prescott. She knows a spell to take you to your room. I've seen her perform it."

Basil shook his head. "There's no need to disturb her. She'd worry needlessly. Leave her to her slumber."

As she suspected, he did not wish to upset his aunt. But, that did not resolve the dilemma that faced them.

How to get him to his room when he used so much effort simply to stand? Whatever ailed him had weakened him.

"Wait," she said. "Can you stand for a moment on your own?"

He nodded. "I can try."

He braced himself on the desk and leaned forward to put some of his weight on the furniture. She slipped around him, grabbed the chair she had used while reading and dragged it over. With a grateful sigh, he slumped into the chair and leaned forward to rest his forehead on the desk.

Julia picked up the candle she dropped earlier. Whispering a few words, a flame sputtered to life on the wick.

Basil lifted his head, looking first at the candle and then to her. The corner of his mouth tilted upward. "You've been practicing."

"I have a certain talent for parlor tricks, nothing more." She shrugged.

He grunted. "You have the blood for it. Your father is a powerful witch, after all. I daresay he's the strongest among us."

"Yes. He had far more talent than I or my sister will ever possess."

Basil stilled. The smile slowly drained away from his face. He looked at her, his brow creased in silent question. She didn't understand. What had she said? What made him look at her with such sadness?

"Julia? Your father? Is Roger…?"

Julia's heart skipped a beat. How had she revealed the truth about her father? From the grief-stricken look on Basil's face, he knew what she had not spoken of to anyone. She thought back to her last statement. Yes, it had slipped from her tongue. She talked of her father in the past tense. At her prolonged silence, Basil closed his eyes and sighed.

"Oh, Julia," he said softly. "I'm so sorry."

She licked her suddenly dry lips and looked away. There was no denying the truth. Not when he saw it written clearly in her eyes without her ever speaking a word. No, Basil knew her too well. Even after all of this time, he could still read every emotion on her face. Well, all the emotion save the one directed solely at him.

From the corner of her eyes, she spotted a decanter of brandy. Normally, she rarely partook of it, but perhaps she needed a drink, after all.

"Julia?" he asked, his hand grasping hers. His thumb caressed the back of her hand. "What happened?"

****

Roger was dead.

Basil's hand tightened over her fingers, squeezing gently. He lowered his head, fighting the dizziness that incessantly plagued him as he focused on the questions swirling in his brain.

That explained her presence here. She had nowhere else to go.

Roger Grey never possessed a head for business. His wife kept the estate running until she died shortly after Julia's eighth year. The estate slowly degenerated into poverty. It became well known that Julia, and her younger sister, Marianne, had no dowries. One of the many reasons Basil made assurances that Julia marry well after he'd gone. George Walters' wealth and head

61

for business, even at the young age of twenty, attracted Basil's interest for Julia's benefit. Basil knew they'd make an excellent match.

But, Julia never married George.

And Roger was dead.

"It...it was his heart," she said, biting her bottom lip. He leaned back to face her. She didn't look into his eyes. Instead, her gaze darted across the floor. She kept something from him. Perhaps she did not wish to discuss her father's failing health.

When she focused on his face, he knew she spoke the truth. "He never got over my mother's death. He grieved for her. So many years he grieved. I think he was ready to go to her."

"But you and your sister..."

Her bottom lip quivered at the mention of her sister, and she turned her head, blinking away the tears that were suddenly in her eyes. Basil's chest tightened with dread. He squeezed her hand and leaned forward.

Oh, no...

"Julia, where's Marianne?"

She bit back a sob. Pain in his chest blossomed. Something happened to her sister. It was his fault. All his fault. He should have made certain George made good on his promises. Basil should have stayed for the wedding, even if it killed him to see the woman he loved married to another man.

Yes, he loved her. Always loved her. He'd known since a child he was meant to be with her. That's why he had to help her, protect her, do all he could for her. Even if it meant keeping away from her.

"Where is she?" he repeated, his voice rising in panic. If something dreadful happened to young

Marianne, Basil would never forgive himself. Julia adored her younger sister. After their mother died in childbirth, Julia had taken to caring for the baby just as a mother would care for her child. Julia and Marianne had a very close relationship that went beyond simply being sisters.

"No, no," she said, wiping at the sudden tears that fell onto her cheeks. "No, Marianne is...she is... Well, she's here. With me."

Basil sighed, relieved to learn Julia's little sister was safe.

"How long has your father been gone?"

"Two years." She held herself straight, her shoulders tense.

He regarded her for a moment, again noting the change in her. She seemed so different from the girl he left behind. Like another woman. The difference reflected in her eyes. The warm gentleness of untried youth had vanished, and in its place resided a serious, worldly gaze. The eyes of a wounded woman. A woman heartsick with grief.

With her father dead, she had no home. No prospects for a decent future or an advantageous marriage. If his aunt had not rescued her from the streets... Basil shuddered to think what might have become of her.

His shudder seemed to restart the shivers that for a moment had subsided.

"Bloody hell!" he muttered as he fought to force his muscles to obey his commands. For a short time in the beginning he managed to delay the shivers, to mask his symptoms and other signs of the disease. But no longer. With each passing year, with the sunset of each day, he grew weaker as the disease grew stronger. And Basil knew what would happen one day, if he didn't find the cure.

"Basil, what is this? What's happened to you?"

He glanced at her face. Her eyes were wide with worry and concern and a trace of fear. That she held any compassion for him at all amazed him. He never gave her any explanation of why he left. He never even said good-bye. She had every right to refuse to ever speak to him again.

Yet, here she stood, by his side, worrying over him.

He sighed. This very situation he had tried to avoid ten years ago. He didn't want anyone to worry over him.

"It's nothing," he said, fighting to sound blasé as if this were such a trivial thing. "Comes and goes. Nothing to fret over, my dear. A good night's rest is all the cure I need."

Oh, if only that were true!

"Basil."

The doubt in her voice cut through his heart. For a moment, he felt weak enough to tell her the truth. He imagined how relieved his shoulders would feel to tell someone else of his troubles, his fears and grief. To share the pain and heartsickness instead of holding it bottled inside him until he burst.

He looked into her green eyes. Such a lovely shade of jade. Like the precious gems he collected during his brief stay in China years ago. The moment he had seen those gems, he'd thought of Julia.

No, he could not burden her with his secrets. She held too much pain already from her father. He would not add to that grief.

"I just need sleep, Jules."

She tilted her head to the side as if to argue.

"I promise you, I'll feel better in the morning."

Julia sighed, heavily. Releasing his hand, she folded her arms across her chest.

"Very well," she said. "And how do you presume to traverse to your room if you cannot walk? I'm not adverse to carrying you, but it might seem awkward if someone should see us."

"I'm a bit much for you, aren't I?" Basil regarded her tiny frame against his larger one. When standing, the top of her head barely touched his chin.

"We'll make do." She placed her hands on her hips with determination. Then her face brightened with an idea. "Unless you know the spell I spoke of? I've seen your aunt use it on those days when her knees ached something terrible. She can disappear and reappear in her room. Do you know the spell?"

He did. It was something he learned years ago. It was also something that took a great deal of strength and concentration. Both, he severely lacked at the moment.

"I do. But, in my condition, I doubt I could muster the strength to transport to the library door let alone the chamber above us."

"Oh," Julia said, crestfallen. Then she rallied. "Well, we do what we must then, shall we?"

He smiled at her determination. "I suppose."

"Come along," she said, holding her hands out. "Best get to it."

He smiled, grimly.

Taking her arm, he allowed her to assist in hoisting him up.

****

It took a great deal of strength to help Basil walk to the doors and into the corridor. He began stumbling just as they arrived at the foot of the stairs. When they stopped at the bottom and looked up, the average, everyday stairs loomed above them like a huge mountain.

"Are you certain about this?" Basil asked, gripping one hand on the banister. His other arm loped around Julia's rather thin shoulders.

"No."

But, with determination, she rallied together and urged him upward, one weary step at a time.

About halfway, his dizziness got the better of him and he stumbled. He crashed down on his knees, taking her with him. Off balance, she slid down two steps before he grasped her hand, keeping her from falling the rest of the way.

"I don't think this is wise," Basil said, admitting he put her in danger with his pride and stubbornness. "Perhaps it's time to call for Parker."

"Absolutely not." Julia stood, brushing her skirts and straightened. "We've made it this far. Why, we're nearly half way."

Basil nodded. If they reached his room, he'd be fine. He didn't even need to make it to the bed. Even if she just shoved him in and closed the door so no one saw his crumpled form in the morning, he'd be forever grateful. Just so Aunt Petunia remained ignorant of her nephew's debilitating illness.

They stumbled the rest of the way up the stairs. Basil did his best to concentrate on lifting one foot in front of the other, of taking each step without falling flat on his face and taking her with him. He did his best *not* to notice how her breast brushed against his chest while she leaned into him, giving him the full support he needed to stand. He did his best *not* to feel her womanly curves rubbing against him. And he tried *not* to inhale too deeply for the air surrounding her was filled with lilacs.

His mind screamed to concentrate on other things, like survival. His heart screamed that survival wasn't living.

He never had the chance to know the feeling of wrapping his hands around her naked waist, pulling her body closer to his, losing himself inside her.

Basil clenched his eyes shut and shuddered, this time for a reason other than this dreaded disease.

He really must focus. This current line of thought was highly inappropriate.

And yet, he couldn't stop fantasizing about her. The entire journey from the stairs, down the hall and to his room, he kept picturing her naked in his arms.

Oh, what a beautiful image!

After an eternity, they finally arrived at his doorstep. He leaned against the frame as she turned the knob and shoved open the door. She took a step forward, about to enter his room when he resisted.

"This is far enough."

Her green gaze looked up, startled.

"However will you reach your bed? Do you plan to crawl?"

"Indeed, I may." As he looked deeply into her eyes, he found sudden difficulty in breathing. She appeared winded, but for a different reason. After dragging his ailing carcass up the bloody stairs, the poor woman was winded. Tendrils of her hair had tumbled free of their restraints and now rested alongside her face, framing her beauty in a way that enchanted him. Tiny beads of sweat formed on her upper lip, and he felt the urge to wipe them away…with his lips. "It isn't proper for a woman to enter a man's bedchamber unless they are wed."

"Under the circumstances, I believe we may forgo propriety," she said, tilting her head to the side as she looked up.

He lifted his hand to curl a soft tendril of her hair around his finger. Her scent drifted over him. He took a deep breath, inhaling the lilac scented soap she used to wash her skin.

Julia gasped.

He looked back to her eyes. Recognition registered in her gaze. And hunger. The same hunger that surely mirrored his own.

Slowly, painfully slowly, his head dipped toward hers. He found he could not convince himself as to why kissing her might be a bad idea. How could it be otherwise? He kissed her when they were younger. What could it hurt to taste her once more?

His lips found hers.

A groan slipped from his throat. Or was it hers? Basil couldn't be certain. All coherent thought left him as she surrendered to his touch. Her hands, which had been on his arm supporting him, now crept along his chest until they wrapped themselves around his neck, drawing him closer.

Her closed mouth now opened, welcoming his tongue to hers, welcoming him home.

Yes, he was, at last, home.

His heart knew, sensed, yearned it.

Basil kissed her deeply while leaning against the wall with trembling legs. He prayed for the strength to continue kissing her a moment longer before his legs collapsed and he tumbled to the floor.

Had he forgotten how wonderful her kisses made him feel? How delicious she tasted?

He found his memory had not served them justice. His heart pounded in a wild rhythm. He pulled her closer so she could feel his heart beating only for her.

Dizziness followed, and before he knew what happened, he slipped to the floor.

They tumbled onto the carpet in his room.

"Oof!" Julia said, as she landed atop him. Basil's head struck the floor and pain spasmed down his back. But, when Julia squirmed over his body, her legs fumbling to find purchase, his pain was forgotten.

He clasped his arms around her, holding her prisoner against his body. She froze and looked into his eyes.

Hunger replaced her surprise, and again she kissed him. This time with her writhing body atop his. Basil barely breathed as she kissed him deeply, hungrily. His hands roamed her womanly terrain, exploring her body from the top of her head, where he gently extracted the pins from her hair, allowing the silky curls to fall covering him like a blanket, then flow along her shoulders and down her back. He found her derriere and pulled her closer, tighter to him, rubbing her along his hardness that she certainly must feel through the thin material of her dress.

Julia broke slightly away from their kiss.

"The door," she whispered, before plunging her

tongue back into his mouth.

Door? What door?

Oh, yes, the bedroom door was still wide open. No need to allow any wandering servants a chance to witness this. With his eyes still closed, his mouth still hungrily devouring hers, he moved his leg over, found the door and kicked it closed.

Then his hands were on her bodice. He slid the fabric down low until one breast popped free from its confines. He took her nipple in his mouth.

"Basil!" she cried, her fingers ravaged his hair, lifting his head to meet her breast.

He suckled her nipple, licking and nibbling. She cried out. When he finished his attentions on that particular breast, he lifted the other free and concentrated his mouth there.

Julia whispered his name over and over, stirring his passions higher with each syllable.

She tossed her head back, her long dark hair whipping in the air above him. His fingers found the fabric of her dress and slowly plucked the fabric upward, exposing her legs. Then he sat up, dragging her legs apart to straddle his waist. She sat on his lap and continued to kiss him. Sometimes her kisses drifted from his mouth to his chin, across his cheek to his ear. Her fingers combed through his hair and down to the remnants of his cravat. Her fingers flickered. She muttered a simple spell to undo the complicated knot, and it was free.

Then she yanked at the rest of his attire. Buttons undone, snaps freed, her fingers pulling and pushing, stretching the cloth across his chest in search for his skin. He tried to assist her. His mind was fogged with desire. He allowed her the control she needed to undress him. When his arm caught in his shirtsleeves, he struggled to free it. She wiggled her fingers again, whispering another spell, and his shirt dropped to the floor.

He had no idea those spells would come into such practical use. He chuckled and smiled against her lips.

And then his smiling vanished as her fingers found the expanse of skin on his chest. She ran her fingers all over him. His turn to groan. Her touch was timid, yet bold. Eager, yet wary. She explored his body for the first time, and he felt as if they had never been apart.

This was his Julia.

His and no other.

Basil's hands caressed the silkiness of her legs, running his fingers from her knees to her thighs. Her fingertips dug into his shoulders when his hand drifted closer to her womanhood. He slid the fabric of her undergarments away until he found the womanly curls at the juncture of her thighs.

She moaned, biting his lip when his fingers reached toward her hot dampness. He brushed against her bud.

She stilled suddenly, her shoulders tightening.

He froze at her response.

Basil opened his eyes. She stared, her cheeks charmingly flushed with passion, her lips swollen from his kisses, and her eyes filled with loving desire.

"I want this," she said, her voice deep and sultry. "I want you."

He needed no further encouragement. He plunged his finger inside of her.

Her eyelids fluttered closed, and her chin lifted upward. Her long hair hung down her back, and he couldn't stop his free hand from tangling in that long luxurious hair. He rocked his other hand against her, thrusting his finger in and out, the muscles of her sex tightened against him. He added another digit, filling her further. She moaned in satisfaction.

He continued, faster and then slow, then fast again until her nails bit into shoulders, and her inner walls grew tight. Her breaths were coming in tiny gasps. When he rubbed his thumb against her swollen bud, she cried out and shuddered. He continued pumping his fingers into her, feeling her muscles clutching, grabbing to keep him inside during her climax.

And then he felt his own climax. He released inside his trousers, wetting the fabric with his seed.

How could he hold back after watching her passionate release? He never saw anything so beautiful.

When she could breathe again, she sagged against him. He gathered her into his arms, leaned back onto the floor and cradled her on his chest. She clung to him, her hands running small delicate circles against his chest.

"Amazing," she said, her voice husky from spent passion. "I never knew it could be so…"

Basil's heart skipped a beat.

"You've never…?"

She lifted her head to look at him.

"Of course not. I've never married."

"No," he said. "Of course not."

She leaned back to gaze more fully into his face. "Did you think I've had previous relations with a man?"

He shrugged. "For ten years, I've imagined you married. For a moment, I forgot you were inexperienced."

She nodded her understanding. "I've often wondered how it would feel to be with a man. I've never imagined doing such with anyone, except…"

She drifted off, her gaze falling to the floor. She bit her lip.

His finger found her chin, drawing her gaze back to focus on him.

"Anyone, except?"

"You."

He inhaled, sharply.

She kissed him again. This time she was more relaxed, more playful. She nibbled at his lips, taking his lip between her teeth and tugging. He chuckled at her playfulness, and his member stirred to life. He sighed with contentment as she kissed him. When she felt him beginning to grow hard again, she found him with her hand. Her fingers skimmed across the length of him.

He broke away from her lips and groaned.

"Oh, Julia," he sighed.

"Perhaps we might make use of the bed this time," she suggested, smiling.

Chapter Five

Julia couldn't imagine her boldness. Basil made her feel like no other. She craved him as she craved no other. For all the years they had been apart, unknowingly, she waited for him. She was made only for him.

She sat up, dragging Basil with her. When she helped him to his feet, he swayed slightly.

Suddenly, Julia remembered his condition. She took his arm around her bare shoulders, letting him lean against her.

"Oh, Basil! I...forgot. I'm sorry."

"No," he said. "Do not apologize."

"But you are ill?"

"A minor inconvenience, I assure you. I'm well enough to continue what we started." He lifted her chin, and his head dipped lower to capture her lips in his kiss. She moaned against him as the tips of her breasts brushed against the bare skin of his chest. Her nipples tightened, and heat again pooled low in her belly.

While he kissed her, she took slow steps, leading him to the bed. Soon her legs brushed against the edge of the mattress. She gently lowered him, crawling atop him as she had on the floor. *Oh, had she truly done that?* She behaved so wantonly! But, he hadn't been disgusted by her behavior. In fact, he seemed to revel in it. She felt relieved by his ready acceptance of her eager passion. She trembled with want of him. After so many years of wanting him, she could take no more. She must have him.

Slowly she slid down, brushing her face against his chest, lingering here and there to kiss his skin. When she found his breeches, she worked at the straps to undo them. With his help, she slipped the damp fabric off. She stood and shimmied out of the remainder of her dress. He lay back on the bed, watching her with his heavy-lidded eyes.

She took a moment to stand and watch him. His feet hung over the edge, his breeches yanked to his boots. She contemplated freeing those tall boots from his feet, but she liked his position well enough.

With seductive slowness, she neared him. She crawled back onto the mattress, running her fingers over the wiry hairs on his legs. Her hand traveled upward until her fingers were cupping the male part of him. He gasped when she cradled him in her hands. Gently, she touched him, stroked him, running her hand up and down the long length of him. Seeing him harden further beneath her touch, she frowned.

He was huge! How could he possibly fit within her?

He sensed her inner turmoil. His hand found the curls atop her head and caressed them. He wrapped a few tendrils around his hand, touching her hair with a gentleness that brought tears to her eyes. He was perfection in every way! How had she ever lived without him for so long?

And then, because her love swelled within her chest near to bursting, she needed to express her love for him in some physical way, so she leaned forward and kissed him.

There.

He gasped.

She looked up, certain she had taken matters too far. This was inappropriate. He must be full of revulsion.

But she was surprised to see his head tilted back onto the bed and a contented smile on his lips.

Shocked, she looked back down. She curled her hand around him, seeing the tip of him moisten. She remembered how Basil's lips had clasped onto her nipples. He had suckled on her breasts, something she enjoyed thoroughly. Perhaps he might enjoy…

Julia kissed him again. He moaned softly, deep in his throat. She smiled, encouraged. She darted her tongue out to taste him. His body tensed, but he didn't pull away from her.

She took him into her mouth.

"Oh, Julia!" he whispered and moaned.

He tasted salty. She liked the feel of his hardness encased in such silky softness. She licked him, wrapping her tongue around him, suckling him. But, she only enjoyed him for a moment before he pulled away.

"Oh, my love, you are too much for me."

Heat flamed Julia's cheeks. Had she read his body wrong? "You did not like…?"

He drew her face up to meet his for a kiss. When his lips came away from hers, he whispered, "I enjoyed it all too much, my dear. I wish to show you the pleasure a man is meant to give a woman. If you continue pleasuring me, I might not have the strength to show you."

Julia smiled with relief.

He turned her onto her back. He parted her legs, exposing her womanhood to his hungry gaze.

"You are so beautiful," he said. His fingers smoothed down and up her legs until his thumb found her bud. She was swollen and wet. She gasped when his thumb circled over her. Her eyes drifted closed, and she turned her head into the pillow.

He stopped. He pulled her chin back to look at him.

"Open your eyes," he said. She did. "I want to see your eyes when I take you."

Her heart pounded in her chest. The heat swelling in her belly lit her body on fire. She writhed with want, need.

She needed him.

Only him.

"Yes," she whispered.

With one hand he lifted her derriere, placing her entrance against his member. The tip of his hardness brushed against her opening.

Slowly, he entered her.

The corded muscles of his shoulders and neck tensed. She watched in amazement as he pushed into her a bit and pulled out. He pushed further in, easing into her, stretching her muscles to accommodate. He did this a few times, and she writhed beneath him, never taking her eyes off of his. Then he thrust all the way.

A slight pain tore her, but he moved again, and the pain turned to pleasure of the most agreeable sort. His rhythm increased, and soon he pumped into her. Her breaths came in gasps. He rocked his hips faster. Her fingers found her breasts, caressing her nipples in the way he had done.

He groaned as he watched her.

Her eyelids drifted closed. Her heart pounded. She gasped for air. A pressure built within her, similar to what she experienced with him on the floor. He coaxed her towards release with each thrust.

And then she was calling his name over and over. Her muscles clenched around him, squeezing him. He cried out, and with one last thrust, his seed spilled inside her. And stars burst beneath her eyelids.

****

The startled sound of a shocked feminine gasp woke Julia. The first thing she saw when she opened her eyelids was her face buried in a pillow not her own. A peculiar musky aroma tickled her nose. She jerked her head up. A masculine groan rumbled from under the sheets beside her.

She turned her head to the right and blinked, certain she was dreaming.

Basil Merriweather lay stretched beside her, a tantalizing view of his naked chest peeking out from under the sheets. Julia tore her gaze from his chest to his face to confirm he still slept.

So, what noise woke her?

"Julia!"

Julia turned to her left to find her sister standing not two feet away, hands on hips, her expression turning shocked surprise to outraged anger and back again. She was at a loss for words as she lifted a hand to point first at Basil and then to herself.

"You...and he..." she said, clearly trying to articulate, but finding it difficult.

Julia sat up, pulling the sheet with her to cover her

bare breasts. The sight perplexed Marianne further.

"Julia!" she exclaimed, her cheeks now flushing scarlet. From anger or embarrassment, Julia could not discern.

"Keep your voice down," Julia whispered, glancing back at Basil. But, he slept undisturbed.

"I won't wake him," Marianne sputtered. "How could I?"

"Oh, yes. Force of habit that," Julia said with a rueful smile.

"*Julia!*"

She sighed. "Yes, dear, I know my own name. Would you please get past the 'Julia' part, and tell me what you want to say."

Marianne clenched her fingers into fists.

"What. Are. You. *Doing*?" she asked, pausing with each word. She added with a nod toward Basil, "With him?"

"I don't see how it's any of your business."

Her sister did not take this statement well. Not at all.

"None of my business? *None of my business?*"

But, now was not the time for this particular discussion. Basil stirred beside her. If she kept up a dialogue, he was bound to wake.

While her sister ranted, Julia slipped with slow and quiet movements out of the bed and searched the dimly lit floor for the remnants of her dress.

Lucky for her, Marianne woke her. It was not yet dawn so the servants were still abed. No one would notice her slipping back into her own bedchamber.

Despite her past relationship with Basil, Julia did not want the world to know she had consummated said relationship. She couldn't even imagine what his aunt might say if she ever discovered Julia's indiscretion. Julia did not wish to trap him into marriage, nor did she wish to be sent packing.

As these thoughts and more tumbled through Julia's passion-sated, sleep-fogged brain, Marianne followed her, waving her arms in wild demonstration as Julia crept across the floor, picking up the pieces of her clothes.

"How could you say this is none of my business. You are my sister! He is...*Basil Merriweather*! Julia, how could you let this happen? This wasn't supposed to happen. You're placing yourself in a precarious situation as it is! *Fornicating* with your old beau is going to complicate things further. Did you not think on that? Did you not take one moment to think what this will do to him when he finds out?"

Julia's brow furrowed, and she flashed her sister a dark glance. "He will not find out."

Marianne stopped her tirade.

"You will not tell him?"

"I cannot. You know I cannot."

"There are ways besides speech," Marianne said. "Perhaps he might help us."

Julia shook her head fiercely. "He cannot help us. I do not wish to involve him."

"He knows where to find it, Julia. He *can* help us."

But, Julia shook her head again, refusing to even consider the thought. She bit her lip to hold back any shouting that might burst from her lips as she told her sister there was no way for Basil to help her.

She did not wish to wake him, however, so she quietly finished gathering her clothes. She made a quick effort to re-attach them to her body in some semblance of her former appearance.

With one last glance at Basil, who continued to sleep soundly, snoring ever so softly, Julia waved for Marianne to follow her. She and her sister quit the room.

****

The corridor outside Basil's bedchamber proved no better for conversation, so Julia instructed her sister to maintain silence as they hurried from his room to Julia's chamber. They said not a word until Julia closed her bedroom door.

After the click confirmed they had privacy once again, Marianne continued on with her tirade, and Julia continued to gainsay her.

"The spell, Julia," Marianne said. "Did you find it yet?"

She shook her head as she sat on the edge of her mattress and stared at the floor. Her stockings hung askew, and her boots were on the wrong feet.

"I found the secret compartment over the fireplace in the drawing room," Julia said. "The books were stashed neatly inside. There were six of them, but the seventh is missing."

"How do you know there's a seventh?"

"*He* told me."

Julia did not need to voice his name since Marianne knew only too well of whom she spoke.

"Where is the seventh grimoire?"

Julia lifted her gaze to stare pointedly at her sister. "I've searched the library and all the rooms where books are placed. It cannot be out in the open. There must be another secret compartment, but I cannot think of where it might be. I've searched and searched. Have you found anything?"

Marianne shook her head. "It does not help when I cannot touch anything."

Julia sighed, rubbing her face with her hands. "It must be here somewhere."

"We're running out of time," Marianne said in an oddly timid voice. "Perhaps if we ask Basil…"

Her back stiffened. "I told you, no."

"Still, he, of all people, would know where to look. He'd know what to do especially when dealing with Drake."

Shivers slid down her spine at the mention of his name. "I told you not to speak his name. I do not like the sound of it. The mere mention makes me feel as though he is watching us."

Marianne let out a sad sigh, though she did glance around the room as if he might appear at any moment.

"Julia, we need help."

But, Julia turned a deaf ear to her sister as she stood and paced the carpeted floor. She needed a plan, something that would help her and save her sister.

****

Julia stood in front of the full-length mirror, holding a tiny mound of bluish powder in her palm. She studied her reflection, staring into the tired eyes of a woman who was out of options. A woman about to bargain with the devil.

Again.

Her stomach tightened with dread, but she gritted her teeth with determination. She needed more time. He must give it to her.

Softly, she blew the powder onto the glass of the

mirror. Then she picked up the piece of paper Drake had given her and read aloud the words he scribbled there. After she finished the incantation, she took a step back and waited.

And waited.

It took several minutes.

The glass of the mirror shifted. The flat hard surface mutated into liquid, liquid that remained on the wall. It rippled and danced liked waves on a lake. She watched, mesmerized until an image began to form in the mirror.

The image of a man.

His hair looked like the wings of a raven, and his blue eyes pierced her soul with icy fire. He held his head high, staring at her with a regal tilt to his chin. At one time, Julia thought him a handsome man, until she discovered the evil that twisted within him.

She shivered as Drake appeared fully.

"You have it?" he asked, his voice deep and powerful.

Julia shook her head. "I need more time."

"Your time is nearly through. I need that spell. You promised to have it by the end of the full moon."

"I promised to *try* to find it," she corrected. "I've done my best. I've discovered several Merriweather grimoires, but none contain the spell you seek."

"Then you must try harder."

"I need more time," Julia said. "I'm having some…difficulty. I must take care how I search so as not to be discovered."

Drake sneered. "One old lady and a few house servants will not detain you. I'm certain you may find a way to search without revealing your true intentions."

"It's not that. There's been…" Julia hesitated. Dare she tell him the news? She did not know how Drake would react. And she feared this man for what he had done to her family.

"Spit it out, woman!"

"Someone else is here," she said finally. She took a deep breath to still her trembling. "I cannot conduct as thorough a search as before since he is certain to take notice of my actions."

"Who?" Drake leaned closer. "Who has arrived?"

Julia bit her lip. She could not tell him. What would he do? She did not want this man to know Basil had returned to England. Though Drake had no reason to hurt him, Julia feared for Basil. She wanted to protect him from the evil in the world.

But, Drake would find the truth out other ways, she was sure. She learned over time Drake would find a way despite all she did to stop him. Drake had methods of discovering things. His spies were everywhere; the birds, the insects, the trees. Who knew what other supernatural creatures he commanded?

"Basil Merriweather." The moment she spoke his name she cringed. *Betrayal!* A knife wrenched in her heart.

"Basil?" Drake repeated, his eyes widening. "Basil? The prodigal son." A slow upward curve of his lips revealed the hideous replica of a smile. "He's the one," he whispered, his eyes seeing naught being lost in deep thought.

Julia gasped. This is what she feared. Drake's attention now focused on Basil. What would he do to him?

"What?" she asked. Her startled cry drew Drake's

attention. He nodded, as if answering to someone she could not see. There was not much in the background other than shadowy darkness. She could nearly feel the coldness from his castle through the mirror's portal.

"Yes, he knows where the book is hidden. He will find it," Drake said. "You must seduce him. Use your womanly spells on him. Make him tell you where to find the book."

Julia shrank back. "No, I would never! How could you suggest such a thing?"

She did not tell him about the mutual seduction last night. It still confused her whether or not she seduced Basil, or he her.

"It matters not to me how you obtain the book, woman, only that you obtain it. Find the spell. Bring it to me. The spell I cast over Marianne will only last so long. After that, your sister is lost to you, forever."

Julia sat speechless while the image of the horrid man faded, and again she looked into her own eyes. Eyes red from weeping.

Marianne appeared behind her. Julia had banished her from the room when she decided to contact Drake.

"What are we to do?"

Julia fought the tears that again threatened. "We will search again. The book is here, and we will find it. Without Basil's help. I do not want him involved."

She suppressed another shiver when she recalled how Drake's eyes lit at the mention of Basil's name.

****

When Basil woke the next morning, he noticed two things simultaneously. Julia was no longer wrapped around him in a naked embrace, and it was no longer morning.

85

The tilt of the sunlight shining unimpeded into his room indicated it was after midday. His growling and aching stomach confirmed it. He squinted his eyes against the sunlight. He could thank his Aunt Petunia for ordering the servants into his bedchamber to open the drapes while he slept. It was her way of telling him he had slept long enough, despite the fact of his over-exhausted journey the previous day.

He held no ill will toward her intentions. It was simply her way.

Basil rose and went about his morning ablutions feeling refreshed and energetic. An odd state, especially after one of his sickly episodes. Usually those lasted for more than a day, sometimes up to a week. They had been occurring for longer lengths, so the brevity of this occurrence surprised him.

Not that he complained. It did make him wonder if the sexual activity he performed late last night had anything to do with this miraculous recovery. If so, he had more to thank Julia for than even she realized.

His hands trembled for a moment, and he glanced at them in alarm. Was it the disease?

No.

He grinned.

The mere thought of Julia made his hands tremble and his heart quicken. He should never have allowed their intimacy last night, but he was a man weakened in heart and soul. Her willing touch soothed an ache inside that he had not known was so deep.

He stood at the door of his bedroom, hand on the knob and hesitated.

How would she react on this day? The day after she lost her virginity.

To him.

Would she blush with happy remembrance? Or would she avoid eye contact with him, embarrassed to have fallen victim to a surge of emotions neither one of them had been prepared for?

Basil sighed.

He loved her.

He'd always loved her.

If things had been different, he'd have married her and had half a dozen babies with her by now.

The thought of children weakened his knees. Children with her gorgeous eyes and curly hair. His chest squeezed painfully. Oh, how he yearned for a family with her.

After taking several deep breaths to control his sudden rampaging emotions, he turned the knob and went out in search of Julia.

The servants led him in several directions. Each had seen her in one room and then another that day. Even Aunt Petunia was certain she'd seen her walking into the conservatory at one point. But, in each room Basil searched he saw no sign of her.

At last, while walking by the drawing room, he heard a muffled curse behind the closed door. He paused, leaning close to listen. A few more oaths and rather loud whispering. Julia's voice to be sure, but with whom was she speaking?

Basil turned the knob without knocking to alert her of his presence. He didn't know why he would do something so ungentlemanly, but he let his instinct lead him.

It had never failed before.

The door swung open on quiet hinges and revealed

a most peculiar scene. Julia, on her hands and knees, peering under Aunt Petunia's favorite sofa. Basil's breath hitched in his chest at the sight of his beloved's derriere posed invitingly in the air. He paused at the doorway, stunned to find Julia in such a position.

Although he was not surprised by his rather masculine appreciation.

"There's nothing under here," Julia proclaimed, and wriggled her bottom again as she swept her hand back and forth.

Basil nearly bit his tongue. His breeches began to feel tight.

"Do you think it might be in another room?" Julia asked.

Did she speak to him? Basil narrowed his eyes as he peered more closely into the room. There was no one else in sight. He opened his mouth to respond, but something alerted her to his presence.

"I know we searched here before, but—wait, what did you say? I did not hear—*oh!*" Julia looked out from beneath the sofa. She must have seen his booted feet standing by the door. She bumped her head as she wriggled out from beneath the sofa to quickly stand and brushed the non-existent dirt away from her skirts.

"I-I-I did not hear you come in," she stammered, a rosy blush blossoming on her cheeks.

"No, I suppose you did not. You were much too busy in conversation with someone who is no longer present."

Julia's gaze darted toward the window. His gaze followed, but he saw no one. When he looked back, she was busy wringing her hands together.

Basil's eyebrow lifted. During their younger days,

he always knew how distressed she was by the way she wrestled with her hands while speaking.

He shoved the door open farther then went to her. He took her clenched fingers into his own and lifted them to his lips. While he placed precise kisses on each of her knuckles, her eyelids fluttered closed, and he found her blushing for another reason. The warmth that spread through him had nothing to do with brandy or wine, but was purely his physical response to Julia Grey.

"Julia," he said, holding her hands between them. "With whom were you speaking?"

She stiffened.

"No one."

"Then what were you looking for beneath the sofa?"

She bit her lip and hesitated before saying, "Nothing."

He tilted his head and grinned. "Why do I feel like Cook when we were children and were just caught sneaking into the pantry to steal sweets?"

Instead of the smile he expected, Julia tugged her hand away from his and took a step back, placing space between them. The gap widened in more than simple physical distance.

He frowned.

"I, ah, misplaced my needlework," she said, still not looking at his face. Her gaze remained locked on some patch of carpeted floor a few paces away. "I thought I might have left it here."

Unless she had practiced a great deal, he knew Julia had no talent with a needle. She proved that once when she attempted to mend a tear in his favorite shirt.

The shirt was irreparable after her good intentioned efforts.

"Julia," he said. "What are you looking for? Truly."

Her gaze wandered over by the window. She shook her head and whispered, "No."

"No? What do you mean? You do not plan to tell me?"

Her head jerked up in surprise, as if she just realized he stood in the room. "No? I mean…I have no idea. Why you would…that is…why would you think I wasn't looking for my needlework?" As she stumbled through her excuse with him, her bottom lip trembled.

His heart hammered in his chest. His gut told him something was very wrong.

"Oh, do you know?" she said, raising one farcical finger to tap thoughtfully on her chin. "I do believe I left that needlework in my room. Why do I not go check? Silly of me really to assume I left it here. Yes, yes, it must be there."

As she babbled, she moved to walk around him, but Basil's hand jerked out and grabbed her arm, stopping her momentum. She halted, and her gaze flew to his.

"Something is wrong, Julia. Why won't you tell me?"

She shook her head. A tingle began on the back of his skull, and shivers sluiced through his shoulders. With one hand on her arm, he turned around quickly, looking throughout the room for any intruder. He saw no one. But, he felt…something.

"Basil?"

Basil shrugged, wishing he could brush the eerie

sensations away.

"I..." He looked around again, certain his eyes deceived him.

There *was* someone in this room. Someone other than Julia and himself.

"Basil?"

"I feel as though someone is watching me." He felt foolish to admit such a thing. It appeared obvious to them both that there was no one else in this room, and yet, the hair on the back of his neck stood on end.

Julia leaned on his arm. He looked over to see her releasing her pent up breath in a huge sigh. Then she focused on something in the center of the room and shook her head infinitesimally.

He looked back and forth between the center of the room and Julia, confused by her reaction to vacant space.

"Julia, what is going on?"

This time when she looked into his eyes, he saw a world of expression. A secret, a devastating secret. Something with which she was reluctant to speak. She wanted to tell him, he could see that plainly with her look of desperation, but something held her back.

The brief moment of vulnerability vanished. She straightened and shook her head.

"I don't know what you mean."

Basil sighed then turned to look back in the room. He scanned over the furnishings and in the corners, but the sun shone brilliantly, the rays reflecting off of the newly fallen snow to brighten the room so no shadows remained. There was no sign of anyone.

And yet…

Basil closed his eyes. He took a deep controlled

breath and grew still. He opened his senses to scan the room, searching for any sign of magical means.

There was spellwork in this room. Strange spellwork. Such as he had never sensed in this house. It left a sour taste in his mouth.

His eyes flew open, and he released Julia's arm as if stung.

"Julia, what did you do?"

"Nothing!" she cried. A small sob escaped her throat. She fought to control her emotions, but Basil was too busy walking through the room to pay her any more attention.

She scrambled after him, following as he circled the room. "What are you doing?"

He ignored her frantic question. Instead, he blocked out the sound of her voice and raised his arms into the air at his sides, his fingers splayed out as he extended his senses to scan the area. His power eased out, like extensions of his fingertips, stretching into the corners of the room, seeking, searching for the source of the magic he sensed.

It was here. Somewhere.

He had sensed it earlier on his arrival, but being that his aunt and siblings practiced magic on a regular basis he'd never given it a second thought.

This room, however, stank with it. He smelled the odor, something strangely like sulfur...

"A spell has been cast in this room," he muttered. A strange spell. Odd. A spell he'd never sensed before, something new. It felt *off* in some way he couldn't explain. Who would be working new magic of this kind in his home? And, in this room in particular. Aunt Petunia worked her spells in the privacy of her rooms upstairs, or sometimes in the gardens, but never in this room. And his siblings each, practiced in their own private settings, places where they could concentrate without the threat of being disturbed. A fairly difficult task with the number of people normally in residence at Merriweather Manor.

He took a step closer to the center of the room where he sensed a surge of power. He shivered as coldness seeped into his skin. It wrapped around his arm, sinking into his flesh, right down to the bone.

This was not right. The magic in his house was always full of warmth and gentleness. Goodness and love.

This magic chilled him to the bone. His heart skipped a beat. There was fear, terror, pain.

This spell was full of darkness.

He stopped walking.

"Julia," he whispered in horror. "You're using black magic?"

Chapter Six

"No!" Julia said, aghast that he would think such a thing. "I never use black magic. Never!"

And it was true. In truth, she wasn't very magical at all. She didn't possess very strong talent. Though she practiced every day, as did they all since childhood, Julia had never succeeded with advanced spells. Her power remained with parlor tricks and simple kitchen spells.

It had never bothered her. She got along quite happily with her small amount of power. It pleased her to help Mrs. Prescott with her garden magic, assisting with the growing of plants and herbs that she used for her kitchen spells.

Power was never what Julia desired.

Until Drake arrived.

Then she desired the necessary power to protect her family.

"Tell him, Julia!" Marianne screamed from the center of the room.

"I cannot!" Julia yelled back to her sister. She clenched her fists as Marianne waved her hands at Basil, desperately seeking his attention, his awareness. Somehow he had sensed her, sensed the power of the magic done to her, of Drake's curse, but Basil did not know Marianne stood in front of him.

He did not see her.

"I should hope you cannot," Basil said, taken aback by Julia's sudden outburst. "Black magic is not to be trifled with. It's dangerous. It will mark your soul in a manner that cannot be undone."

Julia whimpered with frustration. When she spoke to her sister, Basil thought she answered him. She should be accustomed to hearing her sister make remarks and not being able to answer back for fear everyone think her crazy or ask too many questions. Her sister had been cursed for over six months now. And no one in this house knew of their dilemma. She kept it secret for all this time.

All she needed was that spellbook! All of her problems could be fixed with one of the Merriweather grimoires. *Which one?* All Drake wanted was one blasted spell. If she could find the book that contained the necessary spell, he would set her sister free, and all would be well.

"We need help!" Marianne pleaded, tears coursing down her cheeks. "He can help us! Basil can save us!"

Julia silently shook her head in response. She dared not speak to her sister again. Not while Basil stood in the room watching.

Marianne let out a howl of protest and slapped at Basil's arm. He shivered in response and glanced around, searching for the source of the cold air that just assaulted him.

And he would find none.

No one could see Marianne.

No one but Julia…and Drake.

"Julia! *Julia!* Please! I beg you!" Marianne continued to sob, and Julia's heart wrenched to see her sister struck so low. Julia's fingers quaked. She clenched and unclenched her fists. She clenched her fingers, grasping and twisting them with each hand.

Still they continued to shake.

"I can't," Julia said, tears clouded her vision. "I can't. I can't."

"Why?" Marianne screamed, turning toward her. Her pretty face twisted with pain and anguish. "Why do you allow me to suffer? I am a shade. A ghost. My body remains locked away in Drake's castle dungeon while my spirit lingers in this limbo. I cannot touch nor taste. No one but you may hear me speak. I am nothing, Julia! Nothing! And you allow me to remain so!"

Julia trembled, shaking her head. "No, no, no, Marianne," she whispered in response to her sister's accusations. She loved her sister. She wanted to help her. Drake wanted the book. She would find the book. To save Marianne.

But, she could not involve Basil for she loved him, too. What would Drake do to Basil? What if he cursed Basil as he had done to Marianne?

And her father.

At last, the tears fell. She choked back a sob, fighting despair, but the sounds of Marianne's weeping reached her ears. She could contain it no longer.

And then Basil's arms wrapped around her. Julia clutched at his jacket, clinging to him. She sobbed her pain.

It took quite a long time for the tears. She held them in for so long that once one escaped, they flooded loose.

Basil held her close, one hand caressed her back, soothing her as no one had done since before her father died. The thought of her father's death sent her into another wave of fresh tears. She had not cried since her father was taken from her.

And for the first time in over a year, she felt safe. Basil made her feel safe. She buried her face into his shoulder, unmindful of the tearstains that were sure to show on his jacket. She melted into his embrace. The heat of his tenderness warmed her. For just a moment, Julia let her barriers fall, allowed her heart to open and her imagination free reign. For a moment, she allowed herself to believe all would be well, that Basil loved her as she loved him, would protect her from all the evil in the world, and could save her sister.

Relief, like nothing she had ever known, released her. She felt light and free. Happy. Truly happy.

But, reality had a habit of crashing down on her head with the force of a heaving sword. Her precious moments of relief vanished with the sound of someone knocking at the door.

Julia lifted her head from Basil's shoulder. She pushed away from him, alert to the presence of someone who might discover them in such intimacy. He held her fast, the stubborn man, refusing to let her go.

"Well, hello, Basil," Sage Merriweather said, standing in the doorway. He tilted his head, his eyes widening at the sight of the embracing couple. A slow smile spread over his cheeks. "And, Miss Grey, a pleasure to see you once again."

Julia stepped away from Basil, who reluctantly set her free. She swiped her cheeks, hoping to wipe the telltale traces of wetness away. Her legs trembled as she stepped forward to greet Basil's younger brother.

"Mr. Merriweather," she said, forcing a smile of

welcome. She sniffled once, wishing she had a handkerchief nearby. "So happy to see you. When did you arrive?"

"Only just." Sage withdrew a handkerchief from his jacket pocket. Without any remark over her need for the cloth, he handed it to her and sent a questioning glance toward his brother.

Basil remained where he was, silent.

Julia turned and watched as Sage entered the room fully. As she did so, she could see both brothers at once. It took her breath away how handsome these men were. But where Basil was light with golden rays shining from his hair, Sage was dark, with deep browns and reds. They shared the same aristocratic nose and strong chin. Their cheekbones were rather high for men, giving them another reason for the women who fell over them.

And make no mistake, the women must surely fall for them. In all of her days, Julia had never seen any more beautiful than Basil or his siblings.

Julia wiped at her cheeks and nose with Sage's handkerchief, inhaling the sandalwood scent of him. Of the two, Sage was much more exotic than his brother. Basil had once been content to remain in England, to take over his father's estate, to learn his mother's spell craft. Sage had been the adventurer in those days. Eager to leave Meryton, to learn the delights of London. And when that did not appease him, he left for further shores, landing on the Continent and exploring the world.

And then, mysteriously, Basil followed.

The difference being that Sage returned home after a few months of adventuring, and Basil did not.

As if he could read her mind, Basil looked at her. They stared at one another for several moments as Sage rambled on about the weather and nearly being frozen in snow as the storm raged. She saw the query in his gaze. The question she could not answer. And in return, she sent her own question to him with her eyes.

Why did he leave Meryton all those years ago? Why did he leave her?

"I must call for Mrs. Prescott," Julia said, breaking eye contact with Basil and interrupting Sage's lengthy meteorological discourse. "I'm certain she wishes to see you at once." She turned to leave.

"I've spoken with Parker," Sage said, his voice stopping her. "He tells me she is resting. Her afternoon nap, I believe."

Julia's hand tightened around the doorknob. The instinct to flee overwhelmed her.

She thought it difficult before, keeping secrets. First from Mrs. Prescott, then from Basil and now Sage? Was there no end to it? She bit her lip, forcing her mouth closed when she wanted to blurt out the truth. To allow Basil and his family to assist her in her quest to save her sister.

But, in doing so, she would damn them, and she could never live with herself if another suffered because of her actions.

What must be done?

She looked over her shoulder to see Sage, now standing beside his brother. Basil hung his head, looking down as he whispered softly. Julia could only guess he spoke of the embrace Sage witnessed upon entering the room.

"Ah," Sage said, and the sound of surprise in his

voice sent a tremor of awareness through her. Sage lifted his head acknowledging something by the window. "Miss Marianne, I did not see you there. How do you do?"

A chill swept through Julia, and her hand clenched over the doorknob, her nails biting into the brass. Her breath lodged in her chest, choking her, but her body froze as the scene played out before her.

Marianne, who sat crumpled and weeping on the window seat, heard Sage speaking her name. She lifted her head in surprise, her mouth opening to gape at him.

Sage continued to smile, as he awaited Marianne's response.

Basil lifted his head. He looked first at her. But, Julia could not tear her gaze away from Sage and Marianne. For since Marianne did not respond to Sage's greeting, he now took steps closer.

"Why is it, Basil, that I enter the room to find two women weeping? What have you done?"

Basil's gaze swung in turn from Sage, to the window seat, which remained empty to his eyes, then back to Julia, the horror dawning on his face. The dagger of betrayal penetrated her heart.

Sage could see Marianne.

He could see her!

Julia didn't know what sort of power Sage possessed, but he was strong enough to see the spell that tore Marianne's spirit from her flesh. A sudden realization sent Julia into a horrible panic.

Marianne would tell Sage. Tell him what happened.

If she did that...

It was over. Their lives were forfeit.

Julia could think of one thing. Only one thing might save them now.

She turned the doorknob, opened the door and ran.

****

Basil heard Sage's voice, but couldn't quite make out the words. He stood frozen for a moment, staring at the empty space Julia had just occupied.

His brother's arrival had not been all that surprising. After all, he frequently corresponded with Sage, sending his letters to the London house where Aunt Petunia rarely ventured. It was in part Sage's last missive besides his aunt's that had sounded rather desperate and solidified his plans to return to England. Upon reaching Merriweather Manor and realizing he'd have to make the trek to Uncle Arden's to rescue his sisters, Basil knew he'd have to wait for the snowstorm to end before embarking on that journey. He wagered Sage would make an appearance before too long.

Having Sage discover Julia in his embrace, he was sure, must have been rather shocking. Surprising even, but not unexpected. Sage was certain to have remembered the relationship he and Julia shared once long ago.

And Sage sent him a questioning look as he handed her the handkerchief to wipe away her tears. Tears apparently caused by Basil.

"What have you done?" Sage had whispered, while Julia took measured steps toward the door.

"Nothing, I assure you," Basil answered, seconds before Julia announced she would seek out Aunt Petunia.

And then Sage spoke of Marianne.

No…*to* Marianne where Basil saw *no* Marianne.

The cold emanating from the room penetrated Basil's chest, straining to touch his heart.

"Oh, Gods," he said.

He looked into Julia's eyes and the truth shined in her panicked face. When he arrived looking for Julia, she had been speaking to someone. Speaking to an empty room. Or so he thought.

Marianne.

Basil looked over his shoulder as Sage approached the window seat, speaking softly to...nothing. There was nothing to see.

Nothing *his* eyes could see, but something very real to both his brother and Julia.

"Marianne?" Basil spoke her name, questioning his sanity and his brother's eyesight. Was it possible? Julia indicated earlier that her sister was in residence. Although he had yet to see her, he did not think it unusual. Even as children, Marianne was one to run off to enjoy her solitude. Of course, now that he thought on it, he found it odd she did not come down to greet him. Even Marianne would come to greet him after ten years abroad.

Julia fled the room. He let her go. Instead of chasing after her, as his heart wished to do, he walked over to where his brother spoke to the air by the window.

"What are you doing?" Basil asked. He hoped Sage played false, some morbid game, but he knew his brother too well.

Sage spared him a glance. "The poor woman is speechless," he said. "Just what have you been saying to the young ladies to upset them so?"

"What woman?" Basil asked. "I see none."

Sage's brow furrowed. He looked from Basil back to the window seat and back again.

"Are you blind? Marianne is sitting here weeping, and you *don't see her*?" Sage asked, his voice rising in anger. "It's unbelievably rude of you, Basil, to ignore her so. She's clearly distraught."

Basil grasped his brother's shoulder. "No, Sage, I do not *see* her."

The meaning of his words must have shown in his face for Sage gasped.

"Truly?"

Basil nodded, solemnly. What was going on? Was this the black magic he sensed? Marianne was invisible to all but Sage...and Julia.

He tilted his head and considered again. Julia had been talking strangely. As if she spoke to someone who was here...

"Damn," Basil muttered.

Marianne *was* here, cloaked from visibility, and Julia knew. But why did she not say? Why keep it secret?

He turned back to the door, ready to ask Julia the many questions that needed answering, only to find the doorway empty. Yes, she had fled.

"I do believe something is amiss," Sage muttered.

"I agree," Basil said. "We must speak to Julia."

****

Julia ran to the library, nearly flew to the mantel over the fireplace, skidding to a halt just short of tumbling into the flames. She pressed the hidden panel that she stumbled upon weeks ago during her search. When the panel popped open, she yanked the ancient tomes none too gently into her arms. Though there were six, she only managed three.

She shook her head. There was no time to find a sack to carry them in, and she could not risk coming back for the rest. These three would have to do.

Not bothering to close the panel, she hurried from the room, running most awkwardly while hoisting the three heavy tomes up the stairs to her bedroom.

Once inside, she gasped for breath and dumped her burden onto the bed. Grabbing the bottle with the summoning powder, she raced to the full-length ornately framed mirror nailed to the wall.

Quickly, she blew the powder over the glass, speaking the words of the spell all the while praying Drake was nearby to notice.

She was in luck.

Within moments, Drake appeared.

****

"She's been cursed by a necromancer," Sage said.

Chills coursed down Basil's spine. That explained the black magic he sensed, and the reason no one could see Marianne. All except Julia and his brother. He pondered that for only a moment. Now was not the time.

"Why did Julia not speak of this?"

Sage listened. Apparently, Marianne could hear all that was spoken in the room and answered Basil's question.

"She was warned not to speak to anyone, nor seek any assistance. Although her spirit is free to roam as she pleases, the necromancer has Marianne's body. If Julia disobeyed and anyone learned the truth, he can easily end Marianne's life."

"And now we know," Basil said, taking a breath.

"Is Marianne in danger because of it?"

Sage shrugged. "Possibly. She's not certain. She's been begging Julia to ask for our help. She's willing to risk her life for a chance to escape this madness."

"Yes, but Julia would never risk her sister's life." Basil sighed heavily, running a hand over his eyes. "How long has she been cursed?"

"Six months," Sage repeated then flinched. "Good God! With no one to help you? It's no wonder you're willing to risk death!" He moved forward, making an awkward motion with his hands in the air.

Basil frowned.

Sage clenched his fingers and leaned back. "I cannot touch her. I feel the cold as my hand passes through her."

"I felt it earlier," Basil admitted. "She must have tried to touch me."

"There, there," Sage said. "We will help you. Whatever must be done, we will do it." To Basil, he said, "She is sobbing, poor girl. And I cannot hold her to offer any comfort. Never before have I felt so helpless!"

Basil agreed, although he was accustomed to feeling helpless against his own demons.

"What must be done? How is the curse lifted?"

Sage listened.

"A spell. The necromancer is seeking a spell and promises Julia that he will return Marianne's spirit to her body when she finds it." He paused. "He's ordered Julia to search Merriweather Manor. She's been searching for six months to no avail. She cannot find the correct spell."

Basil nodded, remembering his father's spellbook

in the library. "So, that's what she was looking for."

"He says the spell must be found by the end of the full moon. He will not wait any longer. Why, that's tomorrow night."

"This explains her desperation," Basil said. "Come, we must find Julia. We need to discuss what must be done."

"Where do you think she has gone?"

"I have a suspicion she might have gone to the library. She was reading a spellbook there yesterday."

"Let's go," Sage said.

When they arrived at the library, Basil could see clearly that Julia was no longer there. But, she had been.

The secret panel was, of course, opened. Three of his father's books missing.

"Where would she take them?"

Sage listened, then let out a curse. "Marianne tells me she's been communicating with the necromancer through the mirror in her room. It could be she means to bargain with him for her life, using the grimoires. Julia has not found the spell, but she worried she might have skipped a page. She's been going over them every day for weeks."

"If she means to pass them through the mirror…" Basil did not finish his thought. Instead, he ran from the room, daring to hope he could stop Julia in time.

Those books contained valuable, even dangerous, spells that could not be revealed to just any witch, and especially not a necromancer.

He raced for the stairs.

****

"Do you have what I seek?"

"Yes," she lied. She hurried back to the bed, hefted the heavy grimoires back into her arms and waddled over to the mirror with them. "Here."

Drake's eyebrow rose. "You don't know which one?"

"I haven't the time to search thoroughly, but I am assured the spell you seek is in one of these grimoires. It must be. They were stashed away, hidden in a secret panel in the library. And they are old. Very old. Please, Drake," she said, despising herself for the note of pleading in her voice. "I have no more time to search. I've been discovered. Please, you must release Marianne."

"Give them to me," Drake said.

"I don't know the words," she said. She hadn't planned on using the portal. She hoped to have found the spell months ago and planned to travel to Drake's castle to deliver it. She never traveled by mirror portal and preferred not to do so now, even to pass the books through.

However…

The pounding on the door heralded her urgency to overcome any uneasiness. The mirror portal was her only choice.

Basil was here.

Drake spoke the words, and Julia repeated them. The glass of the mirror vibrated, the waves rippling at a maddening rate.

A hand broke through the waves, large masculine fingers uncurled in her direction, seeking the books he desired. She closed her eyes and took a deep breath.

Was this a wise decision? Was this what she needed to do?

Julia could weep for uncertainty. She couldn't trust Drake, but she dare not trust Basil either.

She was alone.

"Julia!" A man's voice yelled from beyond the bedroom door, the pounding continued as he fought to gain entrance. The frame shook. It would only be moments before he broke in.

She handed the volumes over to Drake. Instead of grabbing the spellbooks, his hand grasped her arm and pulled.

****

He pounded on the solid door. Again and again, pausing only to listen to movement inside. At first he heard voices, but it grew silent, and the gnawing worry in his belly grew.

If Julia came to harm…

Basil needed to protect her. Every fiber in his being told him that. And once he held her in his arms again, he did not intend to ever let her go. He was a fool to abandon her all those years ago.

"Julia, open the door!"

Sage skidded to a stop behind him. "Back away," he said and pushed Basil away from the door. Then Sage grasped the doorknob, closed his eyes and whispered an unlocking spell. When he turned his hand, the door opened. He looked at Basil with a smile. "You never could unlock a door like me."

Basil thanked him, then unceremoniously pushed him aside. He stopped just at the threshold.

Julia stood in front of a full-length mirror, grasping a protruding hand. She caught a glimpse of him before the man on the other side yanked her through the portal.

"No! Julia!"

Basil rushed to the mirror, but was too late. She was gone. However, the portal remained open, and he wasted no time in throwing himself into it.

There was no thought in his head other than to save Julia.

"Basil!" He heard Sage's frantic yell as he tumbled through the portal.

He had a moment as he flung himself through that if Reed were here, he'd never hear the end of it. It was not a painful passage, merely uncomfortable. His body stretched, as if his arms and legs were tugged by unseen forces and his torso by another. In the space of two heartbeats, he found entry on the other side of the mirror.

Basil stumbled forward, falling to the ground. He landed hard, his face smacking into stone floor. His body felt oddly disoriented from the passage. Though his brain screamed to launch to his feet, his arms and legs were slow to respond.

He heard male laughter at the same moment booted feet appeared within inches of his face.

"What have we here?" the man said, his voice amused. "I do believe, Miss Grey, he has come to rescue you."

A chill ran through Basil's spine. He knew that voice. It was as well known to him as his own.

"No," Basil whispered, the grief in his heart too much to bear. "It cannot be."

He rolled onto his back, his body still not ready to command more than this simple movement. And once he was there, looking up at the man's face, Basil wished he had remained staring at the stone floor.

Although ten long years passed since he had last

seen Drake, his appearance remained the same, save for the bit of gray acquired along his temples. His face was identical to his memory. His eyes, however, were different. A hardness was there he had never seen before, and Basil understood he looked into the eyes of a man he loved, but did not know. The once blue eyes, always twinkling with merriment, now dulled to an icy color. Cold, hard. There was anger, pain and despair in his gaze despite his chilling laughter.

"Greetings, brother," Drake said. "Welcome home."

Chapter Seven

Sage fell through the mirror portal seconds after Basil appeared. He stumbled over his brother, but had better balance, managing to stay afoot rather than fall to the ground.

"Ah, Sage," Drake said, with an eerie smile. "So glad you've joined us."

He whispered a few words, waved his hand toward his brother and Sage stilled.

Frozen. Unable to move. Bound in spell.

Julia shook with fury.

"This was not part of our bargain." She stepped forward, kneeling beside Basil who continued to stare at his brother. He was shocked. He hadn't known of his younger brother's evil-doing, and she had hoped to protect him from the knowledge. Surely he'd never discover the truth if he hadn't followed her through the portal.

If Drake hadn't pulled her through...

"Drake." Basil moved first his arms, then his legs. Julia helped him to his feet. "What have you done?"

"No time for a reunion, dear brother," the necromancer said. "We've work to do, haven't we, Julia?"

He whispered the words for the binding spell and cast it on Basil. Julia jumped when a shock of electricity sizzled up her arms from her contact with

Basil. The spell hadn't been cast on her, but she felt the effects of it.

Basil stood frozen, unable to move a muscle, unable to speak, even to blink. He was a human statue, able to breathe and live, but no more.

"No, Drake, release them. Send them back. You have what you need. They can do you no harm. Send them back!"

Drake leveled a dark look in her direction. She took a step back, away from him. His raven-colored hair shimmered in the light of the fire burning in the massive hearth where a cauldron hung with a strange bubbling brew. The bones of his face protruded sharply as the shadows played along his skin. The wildness in his gaze gave away the madness that hid within.

Julia barely recognized the Merriweather boy who used to follow Basil around the estate, like a puppy following his master. Drake used to be dedicated to his brothers, to his family. She used to laugh at his silly games, and admire his strong loyalty.

Now...

He was changed. A cruel metamorphosis. Tragedy had claimed him, the death of Susanna had morphed him from goodness and light to darkness and evil. Was redemption possible for such a man? Could he change back?

Julia doubted such a miracle was possible.

"You will help me find the correct formula," he said, his voice a raspy growl more like an animal than a man. "After we've found the spell, I will honor our agreement."

He turned away.

"Truly?" Doubt colored her voice. He turned back,

and Julia saw his face soften somewhat. A glimmer of the man she used to know.

"I may have gone mad, Julia, but I still honor my promises."

She had no choice but to believe him.

****

Basil's arms stretched above him, his wrists bound and chained to a stone wall. He'd been in the Castle Blackmoor, which Drake had inherited years ago. He was in the dungeons, although from the look of it, they had been converted into a laboratory. He remembered Drake had always held a fascination with science and had often tried to blend it with his magic.

His earlier shock had numbed the pain in his heart at discovering his brother was the man manipulating Julia into stealing books that at one time Basil would have gladly handed over to Drake.

But, things had changed while he traveled across the world many miles away from England. Things had changed horribly.

"You were surprised," Drake said. He sat on a bench, leaning over one of the Merriweather grimoires on a table, carefully scanning each page before turning to the next. "They did not tell you."

It wasn't a question, but Basil answered, his mouth clenching around the words.

"They did not."

Drake's mouth tightened. "I do not rank high among our family's gossip mongering. However, I suspected you being the eldest would have been notified of your younger sibling's mysterious deeds. Or did you not ask after me?"

Basil squeezed his eyes shut at the bitter pain in his

brother's voice. No, he had not asked after him, not any of them. He assumed in ignorance his siblings fared well and expected Sage or Aunt Petunia to send word of any trouble. As in the case of Lillian and Melora.

"You were not here to say farewell to Susanna." The pain in Drake's voice pierced Basil's heart. With the mention of his wife's name, pain flickered over his brother's face. In a moment it was gone. "I expected you."

"I…" What excuse could he give? Nothing he said could erase the pain in Drake's heart. Basil had not been here when his brother needed him most. He lived with the knowledge of his failure. He should have been here. "I could not."

"Even Sage, with his ever-present wanderlust, attended her funeral. Where were you?"

Basil shook his head. "It was too late. I received the missive far too late."

"You should have come home anyway."

"I…" Basil said, beginning to make the excuses he continued to ramble on in his mind. He stopped, shaking his head again. "Yes, I should have been here."

And it was true. Wandering the world brought him no closer to any resolution for this disease he suffered. Here he was, ten years later, far longer than he dared admit he might live, and all of this time what had he done? Flitted across the world in search of a myth, a fairytale, a dream.

He should have stayed home. Married Julia, gave her children, and lived happily for at least ten years. Been here for his brother in his hour of need. He could have saved them all from so much pain.

But how was he to have known he'd live longer

than a month? Belit's Curse was vicious, sparing no one of tainted witch blood.

Basil clenched his fists, his nails biting into the palms of his hand. Clever Drake had bound them tightly with cloth before locking the manacles around his wrists and stringing him to the wall. He could not chance Basil using his powers to escape.

He cast a glance around the room, wishing he could see Julia and Sage. But, Drake had taken them away, separating them and effectively halting any chances for escape.

"What do you seek, Drake?" Basil turned to face his brother.

He thought of all Marianne and Julia had suffered in the last six months. He wondered how Julia managed on her own for so long, caring and protecting her sister, only to have Marianne ripped from her and cursed. He thought of the pain and fear she suffered, of the loneliness of not being able to ask for help.

His chest tightened, but he refused to think on her further. He feared he'd be unmanned by his emotions. And he could not give Drake any more of an advantage as he already possessed.

Drake paused in his reading, contemplating, considering. At last, he looked up. "I do not believe you will understand."

"Perhaps, I might help you," Basil suggested, deciding on another tactic. "We are brothers, after all. I should have been here to help before, I know. All I can say is…I ask for forgiveness. I never should have left. My pursuit has been useless. But, I am here now. I can help you."

Drake stood, marking the page in the book with a

piece of leather before walking stealthily towards the wall where he had chained Basil.

"You think you can help me? Do you know how to bring back the dead?"

****

"The dead?"

Surely, he heard incorrectly. Drake could not possibly mean...

Necromancer.

What had Marianne told Sage while they were running to find Julia?

Marianne had been cursed by a necromancer.

Oh, no.

"Drake, I..." Basil said, suddenly fearing how far Drake had gone. He scanned his surroundings, taking note of the strange tools hung on the far wall, of the massive table placed in the center of the room, of the shelf with the dozens of vials and bottles, all containing an assortment of concoctions he couldn't begin to name. Some had herbs and other plants, others were filled with liquids.

And then he spied something he hadn't before.

An arm.

A severed *human* arm.

It was strapped to a smaller table in the corner, with wires from a strange device attached to the fingertips.

Basil's skin grew cold as the blood drained from his face. His stomach churned. He feared he might be sick. He turned away from that object, that piece of evidence that proved without doubt that his brother had gone beyond madness.

He tried to keep his gaze locked onto the fire in the

hearth, but his eyes refused to obey, and he again looked at the arm, staring in horrified fascination.

It was a woman's arm. He could tell by the dainty size of the palm and slender fingers.

Where was the rest of her?

Again he felt ill.

This wasn't a dungeon anymore, he reminded himself. It was a laboratory. Drake performed experiments here. Practiced a combination of science and magic. What sort of experiments did he perform?

Do you know how to bring back the dead?

"What have you done, Drake?"

She's been cursed by a necromancer.

"Oh, dear brother, I haven't done it yet. But, I shall." Drake turned back to the table with the book, then sat and continued reading. "I shall."

Basil desperately searched for the ability to detach. This was not his brother. The Drake Merriweather he had known would not consider these foul deeds. And, yet, now that Basil's eyes had been opened, he began a horrified visual search. And his querying gaze found more evidence of Drake's madness.

A monkey's severed head, empty eyes staring.

Pieces of rock, gems and stones.

A bit of fur, unidentified.

A woman's heart-shaped locket.

Bat's wings, jars filled with dead toads, another jar with snakes, a wolf's tail, a bear's claw, and a dead raven propped on the highest shelf. Still other jars containing things he could not identify, but looked decidedly like...flesh. No other identifiable human body parts, but he shuddered with the knowledge that Blackmoor was filled with plentiful rooms.

"She suffered."

Basil's head jerked at the sound of Drake's voice. His brother continued to study the book, carefully turning the page after scanning it thoroughly. At first he wondered if he had imagined hearing him speak until he continued.

"Nothing could be done. I searched for any spell that might ease her pain. Searched exhaustively for anything to stop the progress of the disease. Finally, I turned to the black arts. Even the darkness could not save her."

Basil remained silent.

Susanna.

Drake's beloved wife.

"I'm so sorry," Basil said. The words sounded pitiful even to his own ears. "Did she suffer long?"

"Fourteen months, six days." Drake shoved his fingers into his long black hair as if he wished to pull the strands savagely from his head. He took a deep breath and lowered his hand to the table. "The last six months were the most terrifying. Her episodes grew longer, more painful. Delirium set in near the end, though she was quite lucid when she died."

A cold shiver rippled across Basil's shoulders. This sounded all too familiar. "What…what did she die from?"

Drake looked up, astonished. "They didn't tell you anything, did they? Keeping secrets is a Merriweather talent, is it not? She suffered from Belit's Curse."

If Basil had not been tied to the wall, there was a good chance his knees would have crumpled beneath him. Tiny black dots prickled his vision as a creeping darkness began to swirl around the edges. He closed his eyes and took several deep breaths, urging his mind to control his body.

Basil had not known of Susanna's condition. Would it matter if he had? Would he have searched more tirelessly? Fighting an unknown expiration date might have spurred him on, but more likely he would have felt guilty for not providing Susanna with the cure. Basil spent the last ten years searching for the same answer Drake apparently had been searching for here. And he came to the same conclusion.

There was no cure for Belit's Curse.

"She died writhing in pain. Dying was a relief."

He would die that way, too. Unless he grew brave enough to end it before it began. Something he considered at times, but found himself too cowardly to give any more thought to.

He accepted that one day very soon his time would end painfully. There was nothing else he could do, but accept it.

"Then she is at peace, brother. She has been welcomed by our ancestors and all who have crossed over into the ever-after before us."

Drake shook his head. "She was taken too soon. She had much to do on this earth yet."

"Her time will come again in the future. She will be reborn into another life—"

"She will be reborn now. In this life. *During my lifetime!*" Drake said, his voice rising with each word. "Death parted us. Cheated us. She was stolen from me, and I will have her back."

"Drake, what you speak of is—"

"Horror? Madness? Sacrilege? I care not for these things." Drake stood again, slamming the bench to the ground in his hurry to stand and face Basil. "Have you never loved someone so completely that you'd be willing to give up your very soul?"

Basil snapped his lips shut, but his eyes betrayed him by flickering to the door where he had last seen Julia.

Drake saw what Basil did not wish him to see. He looked back at the door, as if Julia might appear, summoned by Basil's thoughts.

Drake lowered his voice, speaking with calm softness. "If she died, would you not offer to take her place so she might live?"

Every muscle in Basil's body tightened. The thought of Julia dying sent spasms through his gut. His throat muscles worked. Instead of answering, he looked away.

Basil had accepted his own mortality. He would die. One day, any day. But, the notion of the same happening to Julia sent a bitter taste into his mouth.

He loved her.

Always, he had loved her.

Would he go to such ends to secure her life? Basil grimaced. He rather thought he might. But not if the result caused more death. Julia would never wish for Basil to sacrifice another's life for her. And Susanna would feel the same.

Basil remembered Susanna from their youth. She had been young, full of life, full of light. His memories of her always filled him with happiness because that was her essence. Smiles, laughter, dancing.

She could bring a smile to anyone's countenance, even the most foul could not deny her smile.

And Drake had loved her. She'd brought him

immeasurable happiness. He'd never seen him so happy.

Drake married her...and lost her.

Basil pictured Julia in his mind. Drake sent her to another room where she could search uninterrupted through the spellbooks. He imagined her hovering over the musty tomes. To anyone else, she might appear to be calmly reading. To Basil, to someone close to her, one would see the undue pressure placed on her stiff shoulders. Her hands hidden in her lap away from view beneath the table where she sat, but in his heart Basil knew she wrenched and clasped her fingers.

She was nervous, fearful, frightened.

And, she was beautiful, courageous, and strong.

Basil felt a fool to have left her.

A fool!

He prayed to whatever gods listened that once he was freed of these chains, he would take her in his arms and kiss her senseless. And then he would marry her. Marry her and love her as she deserved to be loved. They would live out whatever time was allotted to them and never regret another precious moment.

With new resolve, he tore at the chains, heaving and pulling. They remained solid and secure.

Drake stepped back.

"You'll not break free of those, my brother. I must admit, I am sorry to have used them on you, but I cannot have you stop me."

"You don't have the spell. Not yet."

"A matter of time." Drake paused, and he knew he thought of Julia searching those books. "Moments even."

"What would I have done to you, Drake? Taken the

books from you? Those grimoires have thousands of spells, some ancient, some new. I can't stop you from looking elsewhere. That spell, if such a spell exists, is certain to be recorded in another book. We are not the sole family of witches who are meticulous with our spells. With your determination, I know you will find it. I cannot stop you. Let me free. I will take Julia and Sage, and we will return to Merriweather Manor. Out of your way. You can do as you please."

"Ah, it's not as simple as that." Drake rubbed the dark stubble that had grown over his chin. "You are correct. The Merriweathers are not the only family to have taken such seriousness with history or craft. I have found others."

Dread grew in the pit of Basil's stomach. He found something…

"The spell is crude, rudimentary. I had hoped to find one more useful, but if I cannot, I must begin somewhere."

He paused in his speech then paced in front of Basil.

"Julia… She is beautiful, is she not?"

Basil's arms tightened, straining against his manacles.

"The spell is dark," Drake continued, ignoring Basil's efforts at freedom. "I cursed Marianne Grey. I used my magic to rip her soul from her body. My wife is a spirit like Marianne. Roaming the earth with no one to see her, speak to her, touch her. She could be in this room at this very moment watching us, trying to communicate. Of course, I can return Marianne's spirit to her body once I find the correct spell. But, if I am to bring Susanna back from the dead, I will need a host. A sacrifice. A body for her spirit to possess. I tried to preserve Susanna's body, knowing I would one day find the correct spell, but Roger Grey prevented me. I couldn't get her to drink the potion in time. Unfortunately, Roger paid dearly for his interference."

"No." The word was whispered, a deep guttural sound that Basil did not recognize as his own though he felt his lips utter it.

"I knew at one time you cared for Julia, but I did not think you would mind, being across the world after all." Drake sighed regretfully. "Now that you are here, I am sorry, brother. I cannot allow you to stop me. I will have my Susanna back. Julia must die to help me."

"No!"

Chapter Eight

Julia bent over the book, scanning each page as quickly and thoroughly as she could. But, she'd been over these. She hadn't seen any spell that might aid Drake in his quest to bring back Susanna or Marianne.

She sighed. With savage aggression, she shoved the book away from her. It slid across the table and fell to the floor. The pages fluttered. The resounding thud as it hit the stone floor echoed in the chamber, and then all was silent.

She had to think. There must be a solution. A way out of this horrid mess. It was difficult enough when she had just Marianne to worry over, now she had inadvertently lured Basil and Sage into this dilemma.

Julia could not allow anyone else to come to harm.

But, what could she do?

She stood, stretched her legs, raised her hands above her head and arched her back. When she was done, she rested her hands on her hips and walked around the chamber, inspecting every angle, every piece of furniture. It was a sparse room, consisting of a bed, an armoire, a desk and a chair. She had made use of the desk and chair. The armoire, however, remained a mystery. Curiosity compelled her to open the drawers and compartments to search for anything she might use to help in an attempt to escape.

Nothing but garments. A woman's trousseau. The

dresses and gowns appeared new, but Julia found nothing to identify the owner.

Feeling defeated, she turned away from the armoire. The view from the single window in the room revealed to her an immense, thick forest. Beautiful, but discouraging. Castle Blackmoor stood in the middle of nowhere. She could not see a single town past the forest of trees. If they did manage to escape, she dared not set out on foot. Not without supplies for a long journey, such as food, water, better footwear. She frowned at her dainty slippers. They would not last her long on such a journey.

Sighing again, she turned and studied the solid oak door. All the doors she had seen as Drake walked with her through the passages and up the stairs appeared like massive wooden fortresses themselves. How could she hope to escape from a locked door such as this?

Finding nothing else to do, she walked to the door, turned the handle and pulled.

To her utter surprise, the door opened with ease.

She stumbled back, her heartbeat jumping, and she suppressed a squeal of delight. Peeking into the corridor outside the chamber, she suspected to see a guard of some sort, blocking her exit, but there was none.

For the first time since finding herself encased in Blackmoor, she felt hope.

Carefully, she opened the door further, peering into the darkness of the corridor, searching for any sign of someone who might stop her from exiting the room. Still, no one.

Did Drake suspect she might not try to escape?

Julia thought not. After all, he had her sister's body locked away somewhere, and without Marianne's body, the curse could not be lifted.

She hesitated at the door.

If she found the spell for Drake, could she trust him to help Marianne?

No.

She couldn't trust him since he held her sister captive, in a manner of speaking.

But, if Julia found Marianne's body, Basil would help her sister with no payments required. Basil would do anything to save Marianne. Now that Basil knew about Drake, there were no more secrets.

With new determination, Julia crept into the corridor. She would find Marianne's body then find Basil and Sage. Hopefully, with their help, they could escape Drake's castle, and the Merriweather's would find a spell to restore her sister spirit to her body.

****

After trying several doors, Julia became discouraged. This castle was a veritable maze with hidden passageways and dozens of doors, some leading to nothing but closets. The only good to come from her search was that she hadn't been discovered.

Yet.

The direction she remembered when Drake escorted her to that chamber was up. She slowly worked her way down any sets of stairs she found. During her stay those years ago when she assisted with Susanna's care, there was never much occasion for Julia to explore the castle. She remained with Susanna who's failing health kept her mostly confined to her room.

At last she came to a door with a thin line of flickering light escaping from underneath. Not certain if she should pursue this particular sign of occupation, she leaned in and placed her ear against the door, listening.

She heard the sound of metal clanging on metal.

A peculiar sound.

Still not enough to determine if Drake stood on the other side, or someone else.

She leaned back and attempted a see-through spell, waving her hands in a circular motion around a small area of the door so she might look into the room without being seen.

The door remained solid.

Julia sighed. As much as she practiced, her talents for witchcraft were sadly lacking. She needed to do this the old-fashioned way. Slowly, she turned the handle of the door, doing her best to not make a sound to draw any unwanted attention. When it was unlatched, she pushed against it, opening it only enough to see inside.

Basil hung on a wall, struggling against chains.

A sound of surprise escaped her lips.

His head shot up, and he saw her. She stood frozen for a moment, shocked to see him in such a state. Then rage coursed through her, boiling her blood.

How dare he!

Drake would chain his own brother. For what purpose? It made no sense, which enraged Julia further.

Without even a glance around the room to search for any other occupants, Julia pushed the door open fully and strode in, never taking her eyes from Basil.

"Julia! You're alive!"

"Of course, I am, you silly man," she said, not contemplating the meaning behind his words for a moment. "But look at you! Strung up like a goose. How dare he, Basil! How dare he!"

She tried to grab the chains to free him. But he was a bit taller than she, not to mention elevated a few inches off of the floor, so she couldn't reach them.

She turned away from him to search for something on which to stand. A stool sat unused in the corner. After retrieving it, she made the attempt again.

"Julia, you must get out of here."

"Yes, and you as well."

She leaned forward, standing on the tips of her toes to where the chain bolted to the wall. Her body brushed against his. Her breasts rubbed against his chest. Her nipples hardened in sudden reaction.

Her gaze locked with his.

The heat in his eyes reflected her own. Impulsively, she dipped her head and placed her lips on his. She kissed him, expressing all of her love in that single act. He returned her kiss, and for a moment, she forgot where they were. Her hands fell to his face, his hair. Her tongue slid into his mouth, dipping, lapping.

When she pulled away, gasping for air, she poured out her heart to him, too.

"Basil, I love you. I've always loved you. And I'm so sorry for getting you into this mess. I never intended to cause any harm to you or your family. I only wanted to help my sister."

"You love me?"

Julia nodded. "I've never stopped loving you."

To her surprise, pain flickered across his face. "Oh, Julia…"

"What?"

"I…I'd hoped you'd forgotten me."

"Why ever would I do that? How could I? Basil, the love we shared was unlike any other. I've continued to love you every moment since the day you left. And I'll love you from now until forever."

"Julia, there's a reason I left. I—"

The echo of a scream in the distance reached their ears. Julia spun around to glance at the door.

It was a male scream.

"Sage," she whispered.

Turning back, she resumed her efforts to free Basil. She said the words for an unlock spell, wriggling her fingers over the lock of the manacles. Then she pulled on them. Nothing. She was never any good at unlock spells, any spells for that matter.

"Stupid lock!" She pulled and pulled. "I can't undo the cloth binding your fingers either. I need something sharp." She turned away to scour the tables for any object with a point to pierce the cloth and rip it free. When she found the dagger with the carved wooden handle, she grabbed it and hurried back to Basil. Standing on the stool, she carefully pierced the fabric, hoping not to hurt Basil in the process. She peeled back the cloth, freeing the fingers of each hand. When she finished, she stepped from the stool. "Try an unlock spell."

"No, I shouldn't," Basil said.

"Of course you should. Go on."

"I…" He hesitated, closing his eyes. After a moment he sighed. "Very well." He whispered some words and wriggled his fingers. "It's not coming free. It must be enchanted."

"Why would he bind your fingers if he enchanted the locks?"

Basil chose not to answer.

Julia set the dagger on the table and climbed back

on the stool, pulling again at the manacles, trying to think of anything that might free him. If she could only unlock it!

"Please, Julia, you must get out of here. Drake has plans. Involving you. Julia, stop. You cannot free me."

"I will not leave you!" she shouted then realized her mistake. Lowering her voice, she said simply, "I cannot leave you." Turning away from him, she jumped from the stool. "He must have a key somewhere." She ran to the tables and searched. Nothing. The bookshelves. Again nothing.

"I'm certain he wouldn't leave the key lying in the open. He most likely has it on his person."

"Then how I am to free you?" She lifted a jar and fought the urge to smash it against the wall. No, it would make too much noise. Carefully, she placed it back on the table.

"Use the mirror. Go back to the manor. Explain to Aunt Petunia. She'll find a way to help. She can contact Hyacinth. My sister was always closest to Drake, perhaps she can talk sense into him."

Julia shook her head, fighting the tears that threatened. It would take too long to fetch Hyacinth Merriweather. Basil needed help now, not in a fortnight. Again she stood helpless to assist those she loved. She clenched her fingers, the nails biting into her palms.

"I should have told Mrs. Prescott to begin with," she said, looking up. The sight of him chained like an animal sickened her. "I should have told you. I should have trusted that you could help me. It was careless to believe I could handle this alone."

"You did what you thought best."

She shook her head. "I've endangered everyone."

"Julia, it's not your fault my brother has turned into a madman. No one anticipated this manner of decline after Susanna died. How could you have known?"

"After my father…" Julia hesitated, fighting the lump in her throat as she thought of her father. "He did not leave me any choice. Basil, Drake killed my father."

"What?"

"That's how my involvement in this began. Drake needed my father's assistance with his spells and experiments. I came to stay with Susanna, to help her near the end when she could no longer help herself. My father thought we could help them. When it became apparent Drake began practicing dark magic, my father wanted none of it. He tried to stop Drake."

"He killed him?"

She nodded. "My father refused to help with his spell. Afterward, Drake approached me about stealing the Merriweather grimoires. He knew no one would give them to him, not after the rumors began about his black magic. He also knew your aunt hired me as her lady's companion. When I refused, he cast a curse over Marianne. If I didn't help him find the books, he would kill her. I had no choice. I don't know what sort of spell he wants, but I know it horrified my father."

"I think I know," Basil said, sighing. "Drake explained his intentions to me. Julia, you're in so much danger here. He has plans. You must escape."

For a moment, she was lost in the past, remembering those last terrible days, finding her father dead in his rooms, smelling the magic on him and knowing he was killed by it. And later, when Marianne went missing, Drake had promised not to harm her, but of course that was a lie.

Basil's words snapped her back to the present.

"Plans? For me?" A cold shiver of fear coursed down her back. "Something other than finding the spell he needs?"

Basil's face darkened. He nodded. No explanation was needed. Julia suspected Drake would not be done with her so easily even if he planned on upholding his end of the bargain by bringing Marianne's spirit back into her body. She knew Drake couldn't be trusted.

"Can your family help my sister?" she asked, needing to hear the answer out loud. This was something she should have asked six months ago, but Drake had promised to end her sister's life if she sought help from anyone, especially his family. She never dared to risk it.

"I do not know, Julia. But I promise you, we will try everything within our power to help her."

Julia nodded. What other choice did she have?

"We must try to get you and Sage out of here."

"No, just go back to the manor. Don't worry about Sage and me. Go!" He tried not to raise his voice, but Julia could see his worry and fear. As much as she wanted to obey his desires, she could not. It was her obligation to find Sage, too. After all, he was an innocent in this, too.

"I'll find Sage." She backed away toward the door. She tried not to let the sight of Basil shaking his head sway her or falter her dwindling courage. "Sage is a wonder at unlocking spells. He'll have you free in no time at all. And then, we'll leave together."

"Julia, please." Basil struggled against the chains, growling deep in his throat.

"I love you, Basil," she said, grabbed the dagger from the table where she placed it and then turned, walking away from him.

"Julia, no!"

But, she left the room, hating the tears that blurred her vision. The fear she might not succeed haunting her. Basil hung helpless, and she was his only chance of escape. She must succeed.

Find Sage.

Have him free Basil.

Then back through the mirror to Merriweather Manor.

It seemed simple enough.

****

Simple? What had she been thinking? A spell of ignorance must have been cast over her, because to find Sage and perform some sort of miracle rescue were clearly beyond Julia's capabilities.

Well, she supposed finding Sage was simple enough. After she wandered the corridors for a bit, she found the easiest way to discover where Drake had imprisoned Sage was to follow the sound of his screams. The noise pierced her, shivers of dread sliding down her back. What was happening to Sage to make him scream so?

After his screams were silenced, her heart leapt into her throat. What did it mean that she could no longer hear him? Was Drake finished torturing his brother or was Sage... She couldn't complete that line of thinking. Instead, she focused on walking down the corridor where she heard Sage last. She held the dagger in her hand, the one she used to cut Basil's bindings from him. It was her only defense against Drake. When she found the door at the end of the corridor, her stomach tightened with dread. She did not want to enter. She did not want to see what had been done to Sage.

But, she had to. Sage was her friend, like a brother to her. He deserved his freedom as much as Basil. She couldn't leave him here.

Before she could reach the door, she heard movement and the door opened. She dove toward an alcove where an ancient tapestry hung and ducked quickly behind it. Julia pressed her back against the wall and did her best to muffle her rapid breathing so as not to be heard. Footsteps echoed in the corridor. Was it Drake? To her luck, whoever it was did not hesitate beside the tapestry, but walked steadily past.

After a moment, Julia peeked around the corner to see the corridor was empty. She caught a whiff of something that smelled faintly of smoke, but saw no visual evidence. Perhaps if it had been Drake, he had carried a torch with him?

Her fingers trembled as she eased open the door. She glanced about, searching for any sign of occupants. At first, she did not see him. The room looked empty. She took a few steps in and found him cowering in the corner of the room, his knees to his chest, his clothes in tatters and his hair smoking.

Yes, smoking. The thin wisps of smoke softly billowed into the air above him, but not a hair on his head looked singed. Not only that, but she smelled it. Her stomach twisted into knots, and she feared she'd succumb to sickness as she felt the contents of her stomach try to make a second appearance.

The odor assaulted her. It was unlike what she

smelled in the corridor. Her nostrils twitched at the pungent odor of burnt hair and flesh, as well as something that reminded her of rotten eggs. A horrid, nasty smell. But, Julia fought her nose, and stomach.

She saw no sign of Drake or anyone else for that matter other than Sage. And she tried not to think of what manner of torture Drake inflicted on his brother that resulted in his current condition.

"Sage?" Julia crept forward, watching for any sign of Drake's return.

When would he return?

She didn't intend to find out.

"Sage?" She spoke his name louder.

He didn't respond. She stepped closer, slowly, wondering again what horror Drake had put him through. He was awake, she was certain. His arms trembled slightly as if he were chilled. He sat with his knees up to his chest and head covered with his arms. He rocked gently, leaning into the corner with his face hidden.

By the time she stood next to him, she worried more about being discovered than disturbing Sage from whatever he tried to block. He must be absorbed in something to keep his mind so focused he couldn't hear her approach.

"Sage," she whispered softly. "Sage, we must hurry."

She knelt beside him and cautiously touched his arm. At the tender contact, Sage recoiled. He flung himself further into the corner, covering his face with his hands. His sudden movement frightened her.

What had Drake done?

"Sage! It's me. Julia."

The sound of her voice must have finally penetrated his pain-fogged brain. She tugged on his hands, gently, trying to uncover his face. At the sight of her, his eyes widened.

"Julia?"

She nodded. "Yes."

"I thought," he said, mumbling something she couldn't quite make out. He shook his head and refocused on her face. "Are you sure it's you?"

"Why, yes, of course!" What an odd thing to say! She would have inquired further, but the memory of Basil hanging in chains prompted her to rush.

"Are you able to stand? Can you walk? We must hurry. I don't know when Drake will be back."

"Hurry. Yes, hurry," Sage said, and his eyes grew glassy. She knew he was lost in some memory so she snapped her fingers in front of his face. Rude, but effective. He refocused on her.

"Can you stand?"

"Yes," he said. She took his arm and helped him to his feet. He wobbled a bit, but was able to stand on his own.

She lifted the ragged torn edges of his once fine white shirt and noticed how dirty it had become as well. When she looked closer she noticed burn marks through the ripped fabric on his chest.

"What has he done to you?" she whispered, not able to keep the horror hidden in her voice. She reached out to inspect the damage, but he grabbed her hand, stopping her.

Sage put a gentle hand to her cheek. "I'm fine. Truly. I'll be fine."

But she suspected he lied when she looked into his

eyes. The laughter that had been so easy to see in his gaze had fled. Her heart cried out for him, for she loved this man as a woman loves her brother.

"Sage," she whispered, her eyes tearing.

"Come. We must hurry, as you said."

He didn't want to discuss what happened. She couldn't blame him. Whatever had been done to him must have been horrible, but there was no physical damage done other than the condition of his clothes and a few burns. The wisps of smoke diminished from the top of his hair, but she saw no sign of anything else marring his skin. No blood, no broken bones, nothing that needed immediate attention.

He held her arm, urging her forward. They ran. Sage relied on Julia to retrace her steps, but she halted halfway when she caught a whiff of lavender.

"What?"

Julia couldn't answer right away. She thought of Marianne. She followed the scent to a door they were passing. She sensed the presence of her sister in there. Julia assumed Marianne had not followed her or the others through the mirror. She thought her sister's spirit safely ensconced at Merriweather Manor awaiting her return. After all, she had not seen neither hide nor hair of her since her arrival. Or was it some sort of magic Drake possessed? Had he some ability to cloak Marianne's spirit from Julia? Dear God, what if Julia could no longer hear or see Marianne? What if all this time her sister had been trying to communicate, and Julia no longer possessed the ability to hear her?

"Marianne?" Julia called softly as she opened the door. She smelled Marianne's perfume, she was certain of it. Marianne always favored lavender, her room at home oft times reeked of it.

As soon as she opened the door she realized she was both wrong and right. Marianne was in the room…and she wasn't.

It was a bedchamber, similar to the one in which Drake had imprisoned her.

A figure lay in the bed.

Julia recognized the bright red curls atop the woman's head.

"Oh, Marianne!" Julia ran to the body and clasped her hands around the fingers. Marianne's body felt warm to the touch. It still breathed, and her heart still beat. But her spirit was not there. Her eyes were open and lifeless.

Julia sobbed to see her sister in such a state.

After a few brief moments, Sage's hand squeezed her shoulder.

She nodded.

"We'll take her with us," he said, pushing her away. Sage carefully lifted Marianne's body into his arms. "Now we truly must hurry. Do you remember the way back to the mirror?"

Julia swiped at the lingering wetness on her cheek.

"Yes, it's in the same room where Basil is chained."

"You left him there? Chained?"

"I had no choice. He's held by manacles to a chain that I cannot unlock. You can free him, and we'll return through the mirror."

Sage abruptly halted, spinning her to face him. His eyes were wide and horror-filled.

"There is no key?"

"We found none. I assume Drake must have it."

"Then we must retrieve the key from Drake."

"Why?" Julia asked. The idea of confronting Drake as an obstacle to their escape sent shivers along her spine. Drake's power had grown beyond mere herbal witch magic. He practiced the arts of a necromancer. Julia had no power in comparison.

"No one surpasses your skill at unlocking spells. Can you not free him?"

"I cannot," he said. His voice trembled as he spoke. "Drake stole my ability to cast magic."

Chapter Nine

Basil heard their voices before they entered the room. The sight of his brother carrying an unconscious Marianne relieved him of his fears, but the sight of Julia made his heart sing. He was not certain how long she'd been absent from his side. It felt as if hours dragged by, torturing him more than anything Drake devised.

"I will not leave him!" Julia yelled. Sage hushed her, looking over his shoulder. When no one appeared behind them, Sage cautiously closed the door with his foot. Then he faced a table, and with his free arm swiped the table clear. Gently he lowered Marianne onto the cleared surface.

Sage looked from Marianne to Basil.

It was as if Drake punched Basil in the gut. The echo of sadness in Sage's eyes haunted Basil. He never saw such an expression on his brother's normally cheerful optimistic face. What had Drake done?

Sage approached Basil, leaving Julia to stand next to Marianne, looking helpless with tears streaming down her pink cheeks.

Basil noticed Sage's attire, or lack of it.

"Are you intending a new fashion statement?" The joke was humorless and in bad taste, but Basil could not think of anything else to say. He recognized the mournful stare in his brother's eyes and suspected he had bad news to bear.

Sage didn't smile. He didn't even acknowledge Basil had spoken. "I cannot free you."

Questions flared through Basil's mind, but he bit them back. They had no time for answers. He nodded. "I understand." Then he glanced at the mirror, nodding his head in that direction. "Go. Take them home."

"No," Julia cried out. She reached Sage's side, pulling on his arm to face her. "Try! We have a moment to try."

Sage solemnly shook his head.

"It's of no use Julia. My power is gone."

Basil inhaled sharply. Drake had stolen Sage's magic. How? Again the questions consumed him, but there was little time. He glanced at the door, expecting to see Drake appear at any moment.

"Try," Julia pleaded.

Sage nodded. He touched the manacles. After whispering the words, he waved his fingers around the lock. When he attempted to pull it free, nothing happened. He swore.

"Go," Basil said. "You'll have time to devise a plan once you're safely home. Just go, now!"

"I will not leave you behind," Julia said, a stubborn tilt to her chin that Basil recognized well.

He turned back to his brother. "You'll have to take her kicking and screaming."

Sage nodded in agreement. "Unfortunately, my arms are already full." He waved to Marianne's body on the table.

"We'll find the key," Julia said. At the look of improbability both men sent her, she huffed at the challenge. "We'll find *a* key. *Any key.* There must be something we can use to unlock this!"

She turned and stalked off to the bookshelves where again she rummaged through the contents, searching for any sign of something they could use to free him.

Basil sighed and flexed the stiff muscles in his arms. His hands had gone numb hours ago, but he tried to wriggle his fingers anyway. It was of no use.

"You have to get her out of here," Basil whispered to his brother as Julia searched in vain.

"She loves you."

"I know. And I love her. She's in danger here."

"We all are," Sage muttered, staring into the air before him, lost in memory. He shuddered, which seemed to awaken him. "Come, Julia. We have no more time. We must leave and we must do it now."

"Aha!" Julia sprang from the stool she had climbed to check the highest shelf. She plucked two pins from her hair. A strand of curls tumbled down her back. "Perhaps we might use this to pry the lock open? Sage, do you know how?"

He took the pins and studied them. He looked doubtfully at the lock and shrugged. "Primitive, but I'll try."

Basil's brother fumbled with the lock, swearing loudly when it didn't open within seconds of the attempt. But he continued to work at it, using the pins in the most effective manner. After what seemed like forever, he at last heard a click. Basil sagged against the wall, dropping to the ground. His brother caught him before he tumbled to the floor. Basil leaned against him, feeling the tiny stabs along his arms as blood flowed freely through his limbs again. He groaned at the pain of stiff muscles.

"Oh, Basil! Basil!" Julia rushed to wrap her arms around him. He inhaled deeply, closing his eyes as her scent washed over him. This was Heaven. He buried his face into her hair and breathed her in.

"Let's hurry." Sage's worried voice broke through their embrace. "I don't want to be here when Drake discovers us missing."

"Too late for that, brother," said a voice from the doorway. Julia gasped, her hold on Basil tightening tenfold.

Basil looked up to see Drake was not alone. Shadow and flame stood beside him, the shape of a man hidden within a mass of fire. His eyes glowed red.

As the first sight of the dark shadowy shape, Sage's feet propelled him backward. He backed into Basil, nearly knocking him over. It was an instinctive reaction. But Sage took great gasping breaths and straightened, grabbing Basil by the arm again to steady him. Together they turned to face their new enemy.

"What is it?" Basil asked, his voice rumbled so low only Sage and Julia could hear.

"A demon," Sage answered, his voice eerily devoid of emotion though he sounded out of breath.

Julia shivered beside him. Basil tightened his arm around her. Glancing at the mirror, he wondered how much time they needed to invoke the mirror spell. How much time to pull everyone through?

"You'll not escape," Drake said, as if reading his mind.

Probably true. Not enough time. But, they were going to try just the same.

"We're finished here, Drake." Basil pulled away from them, standing on his own, unaided. His own bravado gave courage to Sage and Julia. They straightened, and came to stand beside him.

"We're going home. You will not stop us."

"I do not have to stop you," Drake said then shrugged to the dark mass beside him. "My new friend will."

The mass moved forward.

Basil raised his hands in defense, but Sage grabbed them, pushing them down.

"You can't."

"It's a demon, Sage. I don't think I have any choice in the matter. I need to use magic. Whether or not I should are considerations that no longer apply. You cannot help here, after all." Basil's fingers tingled with the power of his magic, ready to be unleashed. It had been so long since he allowed that power to reign free. He understood the consequences he faced by using his abilities. Every time he used magic, it weakened him considerably. It was a gamble to hope he might have enough time to distract this demon long enough for Sage to get Julia and Marianne to safety.

"It feeds on magic," Sage said, quickly. "Don't use any attack magic."

That left Basil rather helpless. "What spells will work?"

"I don't know," Sage said. "All I tried were attack spells, and it only grew stronger."

"Marvelous," Basil muttered, frowning. "Julia, can you open the mirror portal?"

"Yes."

"Then do it. Take Marianne through. Sage and I will distract the demon. If we can't get away, close the portal. Do you understand? I want no objections, Julia.

We cannot allow the demon through."

Julia bit her lip, fighting the urge to argue with him. She wanted to help.

"Your magic ability isn't strong, and you know it. You must get your sister to safety. Think of Marianne."

She nodded, reluctantly.

"Sage," the demon hissed. Sage's hand grabbed Basil's arm, squeezing it tight.

"Don't let her touch you," Sage whispered.

"It's female?"

"It's anything it wants to be," Sage said. Something in his voice, a slight tremor, made Basil look at Sage. His brother's eyes rounded in horror at the entity. His hands trembled. The blood drained from his face.

Sage had been tortured.

Basil's bile rose in his throat, nearly gagging him. Anger surged, pounding in his blood. How could Drake do this? He used this demon against Sage in some horrible manner. Torturing him, his own brother.

"Sage," the demon hissed again. "Are you running away so soon? I thought we were enjoying our time together."

Basil identified the feminine lilt to the sound. The flames licking around shadow shifted, mutating into another shape, one with curves. The flames died away to reveal a tall woman, black hair, pale skin. Beautiful. Mesmerizing. No one might have guessed this woman was a demon until she opened her eyes, revealing a strange red glow that lit the room.

She smiled. An evil smile. Hideous. One that promised pain for her enjoyment.

Basil shivered, and his brother's fingers dug

painfully into his arm.

"I cannot help you with this, my brother," Sage said in a pain-filled whisper. He trembled.

Gods! What had she done to him?

Basil took a step forward, maneuvering himself slightly in front of Sage in a gesture of protection. How did he plan on accomplishing that protection? He hadn't a clue.

But, he needed to do something to give Julia the time she needed to escape.

He took a moment to check on her. She had moved to where her sister's body lay on the table. He glimpsed her as she finished drawing a circle of protection around them.

Good.

She had enough sense to make an effort for defense.

Now it was Basil's turn to attack.

****

Julia had not a moment to lose. After she ran to her sister's side, she found a jar of dirt on the shelf next to the table and used the contents to draw a circle of protection around the table containing her sister. As she drew, she whispered the necessary words to strengthen the circle so Drake nor his demon could break it.

Then she watched the altercation between Basil and the demon.

Helplessly watched.

What could she do? Basil was right. Her power was not strong. She had no prayer of a chance to fight it. She could do naught, but stand and watch.

Like a victim.

She and her sister had been Drake's victims for

long enough. She needed to do something to help Basil.

Think!

The demon spoke to Sage, and its form shifted. It was no longer a mass of fire and darkness. The demon took the shape of a darkly beautiful woman with eyes of flame.

"Come to me, Sage," the demon's voice growled, sultry and seductive. "Let's continue where we left off."

Julia glanced at Sage, who had gone white. Basil stepped in front of him in a protective stance.

How long could Basil hold out? The demon would consume any of his magic. In fact, that must have been how Sage lost his power. When he attacked it in defense, it must have taken his magic. That's why Sage couldn't perform any spells. The demon must be a succubus, draining a witch of his abilities.

A demon also with the ability to control flame. She used her power to hurt Sage, burning him in ways that hurt but didn't mutilate. Perhaps by the orders of Drake? If he had summoned the demon, he had control over it.

Tenuous, at best.

Julia knew never to deal with demons. They had all been taught the dangers since childhood. To summon a demon was black magic. It tainted the soul. Drake's must be as black as midnight.

"Stay back!" Basil held his arms up to ward her off. Not that it would do any good. The demon was strong enough to break Basil's arm.

He tried another tactic.

"I order you, command you, to go back to the flames from whence you came."

The demon laughed, a high tinkling sound sending

shivers through Julia.

"You cannot order me, witch. You must summon me to command me."

"Then I summon you, demon, to do as I bid."

"If only it were so simple. I serve one master at a time. And I have yet to fulfill my duties here. I cannot be summoned until he's finished with me."

Basil cursed.

It took several moments, but Sage recovered his courage, taking a step to stand beside his brother. With a roar, he picked up a chair and threw it at the demon's head. The demon raised an arm. The chair crashed against her arm as if being smashed upon a wall. Then she laughed, flicking her wrist until a small flame shot out of her fingertips, lighting the remainder of the chair Sage still held. He threw it down.

Basil lifted his arms, casting an attack spell upon the demon. Seconds after he unleashed the spell, he grabbed his hand, bent over and grunted in pain.

Sage grabbed his shoulder. "I said no attack spells!"

"Sorry. Instinct."

The demon tilted her head back and laughed. When she readjusted her gaze on the men, she said, "Perhaps I need a new plaything. This one seems nice." She stepped toward Basil.

Julia gasped.

They were going to lose. Basil and Sage hadn't done any damage to the demon and while they were attempting to draw it away from her, Julia was left with Drake standing watch.

He no longer smiled. Instead, he focused his attention on her, as if he couldn't bear to watch what was going to happen to his brothers.

"She will kill them, you know," Julia said. "How can you let her do that?"

Drake shook his head. "She merely wants to play. I ordered her not to maim or kill."

"Play? You mean torture?"

He flinched.

"Drake, you don't have to do this!" Julia said, realizing she had found a spot. A small vulnerable spot. There were feelings hidden in this man, deep within his heart, feelings and memories linked tightly together about his brothers, his family. She knew the witch before he turned necromancer, if Julia could focus on his love for his family, perhaps she might persuade him to let them go.

"They love you. They would never harm you."

He shook his head again. "It's too late, Julia. You cannot stop my plans."

"They are your brothers! How can you let her hurt them?"

"Basil will try to stop me. I cannot allow that to happen."

She sighed. She wouldn't get through the thick stone wall he had built around his heart, his sanity. He'd gone through too much to return to the sweet Drake Merriweather she knew in her youth.

Knowing Drake couldn't touch her while she stood in the circle, she turned back to where Basil and Sage battled the demon. They used any item on the tables or shelves as a weapon. Knives, daggers, books, candles, the table itself. Anything they might use to inflict pain.

Nothing worked. She consumed any spells Basil cast instinctively and easily blocked any attempts at harming her physically. Each time Basil cast a spell, he bent over in pain, grasping at his arm.

Julia could see clearly that Basil was weakening. His movements were sluggish. He wasn't reacting as quickly.

Even Drake took his attention away from her and focused on his brother. His fingers twitched a few times. Was he going to join the demon in her attack? Julia wondered if he no longer felt anything for his brothers. Did he want to watch them die?

Despite what he told her about giving the demon orders, it did not appear that she planned to obey him. She attacked Basil and Sage, using her powers and skill at combat.

"What's wrong with him?" Drake spoke softly. His gaze had narrowed on Basil, studying him, analyzing his sluggish movements. His brow crinkled and his frown deepened. "Why is he losing his strength? She's not feeding on his magic as she did to Sage. Why is he in so much pain?"

Julia watched Basil, too. If what Drake said was true, and the demon wasn't feeding off of Basil's magic, then why was he so affected with each spell he cast?

Her mind flashed back to his arrival through the mirror last night. The weakness, the way his hands shook, the feverish heat to his skin, the haunted pain-filled expression in his eyes when he begged her not to speak of his condition to his aunt. He had needed her help to stand. Then he needed her assistance to climb the stairs.

He had lost his strength, reminding her vividly of Susanna's state when it came time for Drake to carry her downstairs. Or when Julia would help her limp slowly to the window so she might look out upon the garden.

It made perfect, horrible sense.

"Oh, my Gods and Goddesses," Julia whispered. "He suffers from Belit's Curse."

****

He didn't have much time. With every spell he cast, the pain in his hand crept further up his arm. It was sinking its vicious teeth into his chest, making it difficult to breathe.

Oddly, the demon wasn't feeding on his magic as she had done with Sage. Instead, the attack spells seemed to work if for only a moment. The demon stumbled back as he cast, giving Sage time to find another solid weapon to use. Left without his magic, Sage fell vulnerable to the demon's power. She cast spells that Basil blocked with his magical defenses, but his ability to shield his brother was draining more of his energy.

His illness drained him. The more magic he used, the weaker he became. For nearly ten years, he kept his casting to a minimum, only using spells when in dire need to do so, such as now. But in all these years, he'd never been faced with such a foe. He'd never had to use so much of his magic at one time.

Sweat beaded upon his brow, soaking his hair to plaster it against his scalp. His heart pounded with fury in his chest, fighting to keep his body alive.

How much longer until it reached his heart? How long could he sustain this level of magical use before the illness crippled him? Until his heart simply gave up?

The pain was nearly unbearable. It spread quickly through his limbs. With every spell, his blood carried daggers of torture through his veins. He grunted, trying to suppress the agony, knowing that Julia and his brother needed him to keep them safe. They relied on him.

He had to see them through this.

But he knew his body could not take much more. It would not be long now…

****

"Help him, Drake!"

Instead, Drake had gone pale and slowly backed away, shaking his head back and forth. Julia turned back to watch helplessly as the man she loved weakened further still. What could she do? There must be some way to assist him.

Basil used another attack spell that pushed the demon back a few steps. This time instead of focusing on him when he flinched from the pain, Julia watched the demon. And it appeared for a brief moment that the demon lost her focus. Flame rippled along the skin of her arms, licking her, tasting her, enveloping her.

Sage threw another chair, but the demon tossed it away and grabbed his arm, pulling him closer. He screamed as fire lit a path from his arm to his back until his entire body was consumed.

"Sage!" Basil roared, and threw another attack spell at the demon, who calmly allowed the bolt to sink into her flesh without even a glance in his direction. She was too busy focusing on his brother.

The fire continued to lick Sage's body. Surprisingly, it didn't seem to burn. He screamed in agony, but no sign appeared of any damage being done to his skin. The flames simply sat on him, as they did on her.

Fire!

Julia gasped as an idea formed.

The demon controlled fire, was born of flame. Perhaps Julia might help them after all.

She held her breath, judging the distance between her weapon of choice and the demon. As Basil maneuvered the demon closer, Julia broke the circle of protection and leapt toward the cauldron resting over the fire. She didn't even check the contents. She used her magic, casting a spell of strength to help her lift the cauldron, heaving the heavy iron pot. A spurt of energy shot through her veins, pumping the muscles in her arms with the ability to cast the spell and throw the contents of the cauldron onto the demon's head.

The demon screamed and released Sage, who fell away, slamming into a shelf and knocking everything down. The loud clatter and crash of the contents did nothing to smother the sound of the demon's scream.

The water doused the fire and steam rose high from her skin, her arms and head. Her hair melted away, leaving behind clumps of dark strands and mottled skin. She screamed as she stared at her arms, scratching and swiping at the water that coated her, burning her.

Julia backed away, shocked by the horror unfolding. The demon's screams pierced through her, sounding so very human that for a moment Julia was horrified by what she had done. She stared as the demon's flesh peeled away, exposing stark white bone.

The demon lifted its gaze and found the source of its pain. It reached for Julia, running towards her. An inhuman roar escaped its lips.

"No, Julia!" She heard Basil's warning cry, but she was unable to move, frozen in horror.

Sage's fire-filled form appeared, blocking her path. He struck the demon with a fist of flame, and knocked her back against the opposite wall. More crashing occurred as glass containers shattered, splashing liquid along the floor. As Sage took a menacing step forward, his foot contacted the liquid. Flames grew, blossomed from the liquid, and soon the walls were all aglow.

"Julia!" Basil's voice pierced through the roar of fire, the heat of which warmed her skin.

He grabbed her arm and gathered her into his embrace. She clutched at him, holding him tightly, but she couldn't break her gaze from Sage as he continued to burn like a human candle.

"We must leave. Everything's on fire."

Basil's words rumbled low, and she nodded her agreement, wiping her tears against the fabric of his shirt as she buried her face into his chest.

And then he pulled her away, forcing her to look away from Sage and the demon. Drake was nowhere to be seen. She wondered if he fled or was making an attempt to rescue his demon minion. He could be beyond where Sage stood, blocking her view.

It did not matter. She allowed Basil to drag her across the room to the mirror.

"Open the portal, Julia!"

She nodded, numbly. Simply obeying his command, she summoned the spell for the mirror portal to appear. The glass wavered, shaking into what looked like a liquid form. Turning back, Basil gently lifted Marianne's body from the table and carried her to the mirror.

"Go ahead," he said. "We're right behind you."

She nodded, but paused watching as Basil glanced behind to Sage, who stared at the cowering demon.

"Sage! We're leaving!" Basil shouted, his voice quiet in the sudden noise of the room.

But Sage heard his brother's call.

The flames that surrounded Sage softened and slowed. They shrank into his skin until an orange glow emanated from his skin, and soon that faded. Sage stood, his clothes and hair smoking just as he had when Julia found him. But, there were no burn marks, no sign of any harm done.

All except what was hidden in his eyes.

He looked at the demon, taking slow measured steps backward toward the mirror until he stopped at one of the tables. Seeing his family's grimoires, he grabbed them and turned toward the mirror. Knowing that he would follow, she turned to face the mirror and stepped into it.

Chapter Ten

Julia collapsed on the other side of the mirror. Her legs finally succumbed to the trembling that plagued them since the moment she entered Blackmoor. She took in huge lungfuls, realizing the air she had been breathing had become smoky and difficult to inhale. She turned back to watch Basil and Sage appear behind her. Once they were both safely across, Julia spoke the words to seal the mirror, so no one else might pass through. For good measure, as soon as Sage came through he tossed the books to the floor, lifted the mirror, turned it around and placed it against the wall so if Drake attempted to open the portal, he couldn't see in or cross into it.

Basil stumbled toward the bed, gently laying Marianne's body on the soft mattress.

"Ah! You've found me!" Marianne cried. It was good to hear her sister's voice. Marianne hovered over her body and fell on top of it, crying in relief.

Basil turned, not seeing the ghostly image of Marianne, and staggered until he fell to his knees beside Julia. With one hand under her chin, he lifted her face until he could see her clearly. He looked her over, searching for any sign of damage.

"Are you hurt?"

She shook her head.

"Good," he said, and his eyelashes fluttered. He

took several deep breaths. Slowly, he dropped onto the floor, resting his back flat against the carpet. He exhaled deeply, sighing in what sounded like relief to be home and safe.

Julia sighed, too. They had made it back alive and relatively unharmed. And with two out of three of the Merriweather spellbooks. Sage had grabbed them just before coming through the mirror. He set them on the floor and then collapsed into a chair. His head leaned back, and he closed his eyes.

She took Basil's hand in hers and squeezed, rubbing her thumbs in circles along the back. She lifted his hand, pushing the cuffs of his shirtsleeves away from his wrists to inspect the damage done. The manacles had bit into his flesh, tearing into the skin to produce two sets of bloody welts around his wrist.

"This must hurt terribly," she said softly. "We must clean and bandage them."

Basil didn't respond, although she hadn't expected him to. He was clearly exhausted and in need of rest. They all were.

But, something about the way Basil laid on the floor, some stillness that she found odd, made her look more closely. She leaned forward, brushing his hair away from his face. He had a peaceful expression on his face, one she had not seen since their younger days. As if all of the tension had finally left him, and he was filled with comfort. It was strikingly at odds with how he looked when he first settled onto the floor.

"We should get you into a bed. The floor cannot be comfortable," she said, thinking about her suspicions. Belit's Curse was so rare. Could it be possible that two witches in her lifetime would be stricken?

He didn't respond. Not even a grunt of acknowledgement.

"Basil?"

Had he fallen asleep so quickly? She could not imagine how exhausted and drained he must feel.

Still he did not respond. She shook his shoulder, trying to wake him.

"Basil?"

A growing sense of unease grew in the pit of her stomach. Something was not as it should be. Why wasn't he waking? Had Drake or the demon bespelled him just as they were crossing the portal?

"*Basil?*"

Sage sat up, alerted by the sound of panic in her voice. With one glance at his brother, he shoved away from the chair and slid to Basil's side on the floor.

"He's not waking!" Julia said as Sage knelt, putting his head on Basil's chest, listening. He sat back up, his head jerking as if someone had slapped him.

"He's not breathing."

Julia's vision began to swim. She felt light-headed and nauseous.

"What do you mean he's not breathing?" Marianne leapt from her position on the bed. "How can he not be breathing? What happened over there?"

But Sage didn't answer. He grabbed his brother by the shoulders, lifting him, shaking him as if to wake him from his deep slumber. Basil's head lolled forward and back, lifeless.

Lifeless.

Julia's chest tightened so much she couldn't breathe. Gasping for breath, she watched helplessly while Sage attempted to revive his brother.

"Give me your hand," Sage said, grabbing her hand before she had chance to comprehend his meaning. "Marianne, you, too. Give me your hand."

"But, my magic no longer works," she protested.

"Marianne!"

"Yes," she said, scrambling to the floor and placing her hand on Basil's chest.

"Concentrate, all of you!" Sage ordered. He tilted his head back and closed his eyes, his lips moving in silence as he muttered a spell. Julia attempted to calm the panicked screams she heard in her mind and focused on the healing magic Sage was preparing.

A tingling sensation began along where his palm touched her hand until the heat became unbearable.

"Ow, Sage, you're burning me!" Julia said, her eyes snapping open. Sage broke contact, pulling his hand away, his brows furrowed in confusion.

Basil remained unmoving on the floor.

Sage leaned down to listen again at his brother's chest. When he leaned back, he lifted Basil with him. Julia whimpered when Sage slapped him across the face.

"Wake up!" Sage shouted, slapping him again, clearly becoming panicked. "Damn you! Open your eyes!"

A gurgle sounded from Basil's throat. He breathed again, but struggled for consciousness. Sage let out a cry of relief or helplessness, she wasn't certain.

Julia jumped from the floor, and ran to retrieve the smelling salts she kept in the cabinet in her room. She ran them under Basil's nose, hoping this would snap him out of it.

His head jerked away, but his eyelids fluttered

open.

Sage sighed, obviously relieved at Julia's quick thinking. He stood, dragging Basil to his feet.

"Come on," he said, shouting into Basil's ear. "Wake up. That's it."

Basil stumbled on his feet, clinging to Sage's shoulder as if his legs had turned to pudding. His head remained upright and his opened eyes blinked in confusion.

Her heart began to beat again. She rubbed the sore spot on her chest, hoping the ache would fade now that Basil again breathed.

"What happened?" Basil asked, his voice groggy as if he just woke from a full night of deep sleeping.

"You stopped breathing," Sage explained grimly.

Basil groaned, squeezed his eyes closed and put a hand to his forehead. "It's happening…"

"We'll fight it," Sage said, matter-of-factly. "Come, let's get you to your room."

"What's happening?" Julia asked. She ran to the other side of Basil, letting him wrap his arm around her shoulders to help Sage carry him to his room. Basil tried to walk, but it was as if his legs couldn't support his own weight.

She observed neither answered her query. She decided not to pursue her questioning until they arrived at Basil's bedchamber where he collapsed onto the soft mattress. She suspected she knew the truth, but she could not bring herself to speak the words. She'd seen what had happened to Susanna. This looked dreadfully similar. Could she bear it if the same happened to Basil?

"What's happening?" she demanded, watching

Sage remove Basil's boots and swing his legs onto the bed.

"Julia," Basil moaned in distress and grief. The sound pierced her heart. She stepped forward.

"Julia," Sage said, turning to face her. The seriousness displayed on his face stilled her movements. It was unlike Sage to look so solemn. "Will you fetch some hot water and bandages? We must see to his wounds."

Her gaze flashed to Basil's wrists, which were raw and bleeding, then back to Sage's cautious eyes. He expected her to resist, but Basil's wounds needed attention. She nodded. She needed a moment alone to cope with the knowledge of why he must be suffering. There would be time for explanations when she returned.

****

Basil watched Julia leave the room and bit back the sound of her name on his lips. He wanted to call her back. He wanted to keep her close. Now that the end was near, he wanted her at his side for every moment available to them.

But he let her go. She would hurry and return, and then he would explain the truth.

He groaned and looked away from the door. The thought of telling Julia that he was dying sent a chill through him. He closed his eyes, trying to block the image of hurt he would see on her face. But, it didn't go away, only becoming more clear with each passing second.

"You must tell her now," Sage said grimly, as he undid the buttons on Basil's shirt, helping him divest it. With tender movements, Sage gently removed the stained fabric from his arms, being careful to not hurt him too badly. Basil clenched his jaw, not making a sound although the area around his wrists burned and throbbed as if they were alit with flame.

"I can't." Basil choked the words out. The pain from using his magic lingered still. His wrists throbbed. His arms ached. His lungs burned with each breath. And despite his earlier resolve to tell her the truth, to marry her and love her for the rest of his very short life, his courage left him. His end had finally come. How could he bear to see the grief in her eyes? He would carry that vision with him to his grave. But he'd rather his last memories of her be filled with happiness, smiles and laughter. "Take me away from here, Sage. To London."

"Basil, we can't." He crossed the room to the window and pushed back the draperies. "It's snowing. And, I don't think we'd make it to London in time—"

"I don't want her to know." He felt like a whining child, spoiled and used to getting his own way. For ten years he'd avoided telling anyone but two people. Only Reed and Sage. The only reason he'd been forced to tell his brother was the night he'd used his magic to save Sage from being crushed beneath a crumbling wall as it fell apart from an abandoned building. The pain that coursed through his arm and chest had been unbearable and he didn't have the time to compose himself before Sage saw him. He'd demanded an explanation, already guessing what was wrong before he spoke.

"She'll find out the truth." Sage let the curtains fall back into place and returned to his brother's bedside. He sat next to him on the mattress. "It's better she find out now. She can help us find a way to fight this."

"No more fighting. I've tried. For ten years. There is nothing out there that can save me."

"Let her comfort you then. Let your last moments be in peace."

"No."

"Damn you, Basil! When are you going to stop thinking of everyone but yourself? Take some comfort in these last hours. You deserve it and more for what you've been through."

"I love her," he said simply. He couldn't bear to cause her grief.

He had known somewhere within that his time on this earth was nearly finished. When Aunt Petunia sent that missive, demanding his return home, Basil could have dismissed it, written to Sage and placed the responsibility on his brother to handle the situation. Basil knew Aunt Petunia simply needed to try to entice him home as she'd done on numerous occasions. The only reason he allowed her to persuade him was that he felt tired. Very tired.

It was past time to admit there was no cure.

"I know," Sage said, growing calm. "And she loves you. Let her spend as much time with you as is left. Let that be your final gift to her."

Basil's throat tightened. His eyes itched with tears. He nodded. He was selfish to run away yet again instead of telling her what he should have said ten years ago. What a waste those years had been!

He would waste not another second away from her. It seemed sensibility was returning as the pain began to dull. Either that or he was growing accustomed to it.

Sage patted his shoulder then stood. He opened the door as Julia appeared, carrying a bowl of steaming water and fabric over her shoulder.

"I leave him to you, Julia. I find I'm in need of some cleaning up as well." Sage picked at the singed edges of his shirt.

"Oh!" Julia nodded, closing the door behind him. She rested her back against the wood for a moment before taking a deep breath and pushing away from it, taking the items to Basil's bedside.

She set the bowl on the table beside the bed then sat on the mattress next to him. She took a swath of fabric, dipped it into the water, wrung it out and applied it on his wrist. She struggled to focus on her task. Her gaze kept lifting away from his wrist to wander upward, halting at the broad expanse of his bare chest.

Basil couldn't stop the smile from lifting the corners of his mouth. Even in this moment, he enjoyed watching the rosy glow on her cheeks deepen. Enjoyed listening to the hitch in her breath when he brushed his arm, quite purposely, against her breast.

Neither spoke. She cleaned his wounds. He watched her.

As soon as his wrists were wrapped securely in clean bandages, he grabbed her arm and pulled her roughly on top of him. She surrendered to his kiss as he gathered her so she rested along his length in the bed. He was already hard from watching her, and she felt it. She rocked her hips gently against him. He groaned, his hands seeking her buttocks to clasp her harder against him.

She broke away from his lips to place tender kisses along his cheek, her tongue tracing the curve of his ear. She continued across the length of his neck and onto his chest where she worshipped him by kissing, licking and touching every inch of exposed skin. And during it all, she continued to rock against him, rubbing herself along his manhood, until the pressure began building, and he feared he would not last much longer.

Her breathing was fast and deep as though she had run for miles and miles. At last, she looked up, the pleasure in her eyes deepening the color around her irises.

"I cannot wait," she said, sliding off of him. She ripped at her under garments, kicking them free while gathering up her dress to wrap her legs around him. She undid the laces on his breeches and yanked them down so his member sprang free, alert and ready. She raised herself up, and he helped guide her onto him.

Basil moaned at the hot, wet silk encasing him, squeezing around him. She paused for a moment, adjusting to the size of him, and then she rocked her hips, sliding up and down in slow, sure strokes.

She kept her hands on his chest for balance as she learned the motions to this new dance. He took the opportunity to unlace the top of her dress, tugging the fabric down to expose her breasts. He cupped them, squeezing and caressing while she closed her eyes and tossed back her head.

Their coupling did not last long, each eager to express in physical form the feelings building between them. The last several hours spent not knowing the fate of one another also pushed them over the edge, as they took this moment to give thanks that they both survived this latest ordeal.

Upon completion, Julia fell upon Basil's chest, her hair spilling over him, shrouding them both. He ran his fingers through the silky strands, liking the texture against his skin.

If only he could have forever with her.

"I love you, Julia."

Her arms tightened around him, gathering him closer as if she planned to never let him go again. "Oh, Basil," she said, his name falling from her lips like a sigh. "I've waited so long to hear you say that."

"I'm sorry I've wasted so much time. I was fool. I was searching for…something." *Ah, Gods!* He cringed, still having difficulty saying the words.

"Did you find it?"

"I did not."

"Do you plan to continue your search?"

He let out a sigh, her body moving with the rhythm of his breathing. "No."

She lifted her head, placing her chin on her folded hands on his chest. She smiled. "Good. I missed you terribly while you were gone."

Little else could send shooting pains through his heart than those words or the expression of happiness and contentment on her face.

He must have showed his discomfort, for her head jerked up. "What?"

Basil looked away. *Coward*! He couldn't even bring himself to look into her eyes. Suddenly the wall of his bedchamber looked most interesting.

"Basil? Are you leaving again?"

This was it. He could delay it no longer. He forced his gaze back to hers. He lifted his hand to brush the hair away from her face. Ah, what a face! She was such a beauty with her fair skin and green eyes. He wanted to memorize each feature, to never forget what she looked like in this moment, to carry an image of her seared in his mind even into the afterlife.

"Not willingly," he said in answer to her question. He kept his voice calm, serene even, as he continued. "Julia, there's something I should have told you a long time ago. I'm dying."

The words tasted like dust. He kept his gaze on her, watching her reaction. Trying to prepare his heart for her anger, her dismay, her hate. Yes, that's what he feared the most. He didn't realize it until that moment. He was afraid. What if she left him? What if when she learned he had this most horrible disease, she would cut ties with him rather than watch him suffer until the end?

But, she just stared. For several moments, she studied his face. Measuring the look in his eyes perhaps? He didn't know what exactly she looked for, but his heart thumped wildly, waiting for her answer.

"I know," she said, her voice calm and serene.

"You know?" Again, the dust smothered him as he spoke. He needed a drink, a stiff drink. Soon. He wondered if Sage would return with a bottle in anticipation of his needs.

"The," Julia began, but faltered. She studied him again, although her eyes had widened a bit. Her fingers tightened into fists on his chest.

He gave her the time she needed to continue. She said she knew of his condition. Had she guessed it when he needed her help to stand last night? There must be any number of reasons for his condition upon his arrival last night. At the moment, he couldn't think of any save the truth. But, how had she guessed it?

He waited for her to continue and while he did, he studied every feature of her face, every curve, every pore on her perfect skin. He smiled as he admired her beauty.

"I recognized the symptoms. Susanna had…it," Julia said, unwilling to say the name of the disease that claimed the woman's life. "I stayed with her, did you know? Until the very end. That's what drove Drake to insanity. His wife meant everything to him and he tried beyond all measure to save her."

She paused for a moment.

"How long have you had it?" she asked, nearly choking on the words. *Ah, the dust has settled in her mouth, too.*

"Ten years."

Her eyes lit with understanding. "That's why you left."

He nodded. "I thought to find a cure. I've been to every witch and sorcerer I could find. I've followed every clue and rumor. I've traveled to four continents, into jungles and deserts. Into crowded cities and the remotest villages. I've found an herb that suppresses the condition, perhaps prolongs life a bit, but no cure. In fact, I never expected to live even this long."

"Then you never planned to return, did you?"

He shook his head. "How could I? When all I could give you was grief? You know typically after the first signs of the disease, the sufferer will last only a few months, maybe a few years. Little did I know the herb I found would help prolong it. But the symptoms continued unabated. My episodes are more frequent and last longer each time. It will not be much longer."

"How long, do you think?"

Basil shrugged, twirling a lock of her hair around his finger. "Days. Maybe weeks. Not more than that, I fear."

"Weeks," she whispered, her eyes going distant as she stared solemnly into nothing for a while. A tear glistened in the corner of her eye.

This was it. Now, she will rage for not telling her sooner. For lying.

But, she shook her head, as if snapping out of the trance she had succumbed to.

To his utter surprise, she smiled. "Well, then we'd better make the most of the time left to us."

She lowered her head and kissed him. Basil lost himself for several heated moments, but at last he pulled away to look up.

"You do not hate me? You're not going to scream in rage because I lied?"

"I could never hate you, Basil," Julia said, stroking his chin with her fingertip. "And what good would screaming or crying do? If my tears would cure you, I'd cry enough to fill oceans. But, it will do no good. I'll weep for you, this is true. At some moment I must. But, if we have only a brief time together, then I'm not about to waste precious moments on tears. I'd rather spend it loving you, showing my love for you, loving you enough to last a lifetime."

"Oh, Julia," he said then sighed. "Marry me, Julia. Be my wife."

She nodded, smiling and again tears shimmered at the corners of her eyes. "Yes, my love. Yes."

Chapter Eleven

Several days later, Julia had just finished pouring tea at the table by Basil's bedside when Mrs. Prescott entered, gathering her shawl close around her shoulders.

"You have a caller, Basil," Mrs. Prescott said upon entering. "I've just encountered Parker on the stairs. He tells me there is a man here to see you."

"Did he give his name?"

"A Mr. Reed, he tells me."

Basil straightened, a broad smile lighting his face. "Indeed?"

"Shall I have Parker bring him up?"

"Yes, please do," he answered, the grin never leaving his face. Mrs. Prescott nodded her approval and stepped out to speak with Parker who hovered by the doorway.

Julia leaned forward. "Who is Mr. Reed?"

"He's my assistant. I found him in Belgium about six years ago about to be beaten to death by a band of ruffians. I intervened and saved his life. He returned the favor by saving mine, more than once I might add."

"Oh," Julia said, leaning back as Mrs. Prescott re-entered the room.

"I've spoken with the girls. Melora was finally able to find a mirror to use for contact," she said and lowered herself into her favorite chair which the servants had moved up from the library several days ago. Julia poured another cup of tea, preparing it the way the dear old lady liked it.

"And how do they do?" Basil asked, carefully sipping the hot liquid while sitting propped up by pillows in his bed. His hand trembled as he lowered the teacup. "Do they still need rescuing? Since the snow has finally stopped, Sage can ready the horses and be on his way in an hour's time."

"Oh, Basil. Would he, do you think?" Aunt Petunia asked. "I won't rest easy until they're home safe."

"Of course, though it'll be a few days before he can get them home. Uncle Arden's estate is at least two days journey south of here. And I suppose he'll have a few words to say about their departure."

"Oh, no, Sage won't have to travel there, after all. They're staying at a house west of here. Caldwell House."

"Caldwell? Never heard of it."

"It's owned by a Mr. Collins."

"Well, how the devil did they end up there?"

"It's a long story. Each has their tale to tell. But, here's the thing, Basil, which has me out of sorts with worry. They're both in love."

"With Mr. Collins?"

"No, no," she said, waving her hands at his misinterpretation. "Melora says she's in love with Mr. Collins, and Lillian is to marry Lord North."

"North? I haven't heard of him either."

"I have," Julia said, joining the conversation. She set her cup of tea on the tray. "Lord Jeremy North is very handsome, I hear." She smiled as Basil slanted a look her way. "And very wealthy. He's quite a catch, they say."

"Do they?" Basil muttered, staring into the bottom of his teacup. Was he wishing for something a little stronger than tea?

"He does, however, have some odd habits, they also say. He sends his entire staff on holiday once a month, every month."

"Must be an eccentric," Mrs. Prescott added.

"Indeed," Basil muttered again.

Julia glanced his way. He still seemed disgruntled over her 'handsome' remark. She reached for him, wrapping her slender fingers around his hand.

"You're much better looking, Mr. Merriweather," she whispered as Mrs. Prescott launched into a long list of reasons why his sisters needed to be delivered home at once.

He grinned, and Julia realized he must have been funning her. He clasped her hand. She blushed, but did not worry over any comment Mrs. Prescott might utter. They explained their intentions to her on the same day they returned from Drake's castle.

She had been happy beyond belief, especially when Basil informed her that he intended to remain at Merriweather Manor and halt his world-traveling. He did have to explain the other reasons he intended to stay, and he would have waited a day or so before he approached her about it. But, his illness grew worse. He had no choice but to explain why he had such difficulty standing without assistance.

His aunt had been upset, considerably at first, but later she admitted she suspected something of the sort. Basil had never been one for travel when he was young, more the responsible sort that stayed home to see to family. When he left and didn't immediately return, her heart told her something was amiss.

Julia wasn't sure if what his aunt said was true, or if she merely wished to take the weight of guilt from his shoulders. He was sensitive about those in his family since he loved them dearly.

She gave his hand another squeeze before pouring more tea.

"I haven't even told you the worst," Mrs. Prescott said, oblivious to the heated looks Julia received from Basil, and she to him.

"I implore you, Aunt, tell us all," Basil said, grinning at Julia. She doubted he'd heard a word of his aunt's dissertation. He'd spent the last few moments ogling her in such a way Julia couldn't stop from imagining what he intended later. He was certain to demand she sneak into his room, as she had every night since they promised to marry. On the nights he had no strength to express his love in a physical manner, they would hold each other close before drifting off to sleep.

"Well, Melora tells me, and I must beg secrecy from the both of you, but of course you can keep secrets especially regarding family, and just the way your sister went on about this man, I'm all but certain he will become family in a short while, but I'm getting ahead of myself. What was I saying?"

"Melora says…" Julia prompted.

"Ah, yes! But, not Melora. No, it's about Mr. Collins. He's…" She paused, leaning forward to whisper the word. "A vampire."

Basil snorted into his tea.

Julia jumped in surprise and grabbed a cloth to help him wipe the tea away from his mouth, nose and chin.

He coughed, sputtered and laughed, taking the cloth and wiping his face.

"You cannot be serious," he said.

"Did I not teach you about such creatures, my boy?" Mrs. Prescott asked, scolding. "Then again, you and your brothers were never ones to sit still long enough for some of my lessons. It was a wonder you learned any spells at all."

"But, vampires are mythological," Julia said. Unlike Basil, she remembered her lessons. While the boys manifested frogs to put on their sister's beds at night, she actually studied and worked on growing her practically non-existent powers.

"No, they're quite real," Basil said, his coughing subsided. "I met a few during my travels."

Julia gasped, then shuddered. "Are they not evil creatures?"

"Certainly not," he explained. "They were human once. When they are turned, they take on many of the traits they had as humans. Only if they were evil humans, will they be evil as vampires."

"Melora wouldn't fall in love with anyone of that nature, I'm certain," Julia said to Mrs. Prescott, hoping to alleviate the old woman's worries.

"No, no, you are right. I suppose he must have some redeeming qualities for her to love him."

"Then why are you so upset?"

"I had hoped both of your sisters might find a nice witch to settle down with, maybe even a sorcerer. I knew no good would come sending them off to my brother's estate."

"Well, Lord North sounds like a good sort," Basil said. "I suppose you should be happy Lillian has found someone, though not of witch blood, at least he's not a vampire."

"No," Mrs. Prescott said. "But, Melora mentioned we had some spell work to do for him. Something in the spring. I have my suspicions."

"Quit your worries, dear aunt," Basil said, smiling. "All will end well, I'm certain."

A knock at the door ended their conversation and by Basil's command the door opened to reveal a man with brown hair and deep blue eyes, dressed in coordinating colors of brown and tan. At first glance, the man appeared to be an ordinary commoner, his clothes well-worn and stitched with care in places that were previously torn. With nothing unusual or outstanding about him, Julia did not notice at first the glint of intelligence in his eyes. Seeing it now, she also noticed his proud stature, the confident way he held his fit and trim body and the way his bright gaze assessed each occupant in the room with calculated measure.

"Reed!" Basil shouted, swinging his legs out from where he reclined on the bed and moved to stand. Julia raised her hand to his arm, about to stop him before he tried to rise. He had done the same the day before only to have his legs collapse beneath him, sending him crashing to the floor. Her chest tightened at the reminder of how rapidly his condition was worsening.

Again, Basil attempted to stand, forgetting in his excitement at the sight of his friend that his weakened body would no longer support his weight. Julia grabbed his arm, just as his legs folded under, but he caught the edge of the bed, lowering himself back onto the mattress.

"Damn," he muttered, flushing with embarrassment

at his inability.

Reed walked slowly into the room, his hands clutching a satchel that looked as worn out as his clothes.

"Been using magic again, have you?" Reed asked, a note of disapproval in his deep voice.

Basil waved a dismissive hand. "Hardly," he lied, but Julia could see that Reed's eyes had darkened at the state of Basil's health.

"I let you part from my side for a few days and you're off casting spells willy nilly," Reed said, a sad smile curved the corners of his lips for a moment before he looked with alarm at Julia. "Or is this solely from traveling through the mirror?"

Julia gave a quick shake of her head, wondering if he knew of her, if Basil had talked of her at all during his many years as this man's companion.

"I'm fine," Basil barked, rearranging himself on the bed with a scowl. Julia had learned much in the last few days about Basil's temperament regarding his illness. He did not like to be fussed over. For the most part, he tried to go about his day as though all was well. In the mornings, he had the strength to get from bed and walked unaided downstairs for breakfast, but shortly after midday, his limbs grew weak. Julia was grateful he was not yet confined to bed, but she worried how he would feel when the day arrived. He despised being treated as an invalid.

Reed grunted at Basil's response, but Basil chose not to regard it. Instead, he went about introductions. Julia and Mrs. Prescott nodded and greeted him appropriately.

Reed's gaze lingered on Julia, a light appearing in

those dark depths after Basil mentioned her name. Julia's suspicions were confirmed.

He *had* talked of her.

"You arrived faster than I expected," Basil said.

Reed shrugged, but Julia saw his shoulders tense at the observation. "I worried."

Basil frowned, but Reed continued before he could make any argument. "We traveled west for a few days before coming across an elderly gentlemen and his wife. They were kind enough to give us shelter during a storm that hit the area. During our stay, I discovered the wife was a witch. She agreed to allow us to travel through mirror to her brother's home in London."

"How fares Mary and the babe?"

Reed nodded, taking another step into the room. "Well. They are both well. They remain in London."

"You must bring them here," Basil said. "We'll send a carriage at once. You must stay with us."

"I thank you," Reed said, the tension in his face relaxing a bit. He reached out to Basil, handing the satchel to him. "I brought your books and notes. Seems you may still have need of them."

****

The next day, Sage burst into Basil's bedchamber followed by Marianne and Reed. Julia frowned at the sight of her sister. They still hadn't found a cure for Marianne. Even Mrs. Prescott was at a loss when they explained what Drake had done to the poor girl.

Sage had been busy studying the grimoires he brought back from Drake's castle, trying to find something she missed. After Mr. Reed's arrival yesterday, they two had been closed in the library studying medicinal books and incantations, searching for any clue that may lead them to a cure for Basil. Or at the very least, something to alleviate the symptoms of the disease. Basil had given up hope that any such spell or cure might exist and he urged them to stop wasting their time. They also searched for any spells that might bring about the reunion of Marianne's spirit with her body. If Drake had found a spell to split them, there must be a spell to bring them together.

"I can't believe we've found it," Sage said, rushing into the room, carrying one of the heavy tomes open to a page in which he had placed his finger.

"A spell for Marianne?" Julia asked, eager to hear the good news.

"No," Marianne said, sullenly. "But, it's not for lack of trying. He's been reading for days. He promises not to give up searching."

"Oh," Julia said, sighing. "Then what *did* you find?"

"A cure for Basil."

Julia gasped. Silence fell in the room. She looked at Basil to see he'd grown a shade paler than normal, and she readied herself to catch him if he fainted.

"Are you certain?" he asked, moving his mouth as if it were suddenly dry as sand.

Sage's eyes were wide with excitement. He fairly danced on the carpet, he couldn't keep his feet standing still.

"Yes," he said and nodded. "Yes!"

"But…how? I searched those grimoires the year before I left home. I hoped I'd find something to help me, but there was nothing."

"This isn't one of the Merriweather grimoires," Sage explained, moving the book to expose the cover to their view. "I grabbed one of Drake's spellbooks, thinking it one of ours."

"Drake had this spell?" Julia asked, leaning forward in her seat. "But, if he had this, why didn't he use it for his wife?"

Sage shook his head. "I don't know. Maybe he never thought to look for it, or perhaps he didn't have it when she needed it. He might have discovered it after..." Sage didn't finish, and his merriment became subdued at the mention of his sister-in-law's death.

"It's only part of the cure," Reed added, drawing attention to where he stood hovering behind. "We've found there's a combination. Part of it you are responsible for, Mr. Merriweather. That herb you found in France. The one that's extended your life despite the illness. It's one of the ingredients."

"And we have it," Sage added. "Mr. Reed brought some home. Basil can be saved. There's just one more thing," Sage said, dragging a chair closer and sitting. He placed the book on the table and read aloud more of the ingredients for the spell. Most were rare, but not unobtainable.

"Except," Sage said, grimly. "It calls for three drops of vampire blood. I don't know where we might find a vampire in England."

Julia lifted her head from the book and looked from Basil to Mrs. Prescott, each sharing a shocked demeanor. They stared at each other for a moment in silence, their conversation from yesterday returning to their minds.

"And to find one willing to share his blood," Sage said, shoving the book away and leaning back. "Well, I know this is most likely impossible. But, perhaps we might substitute it with something else. Surely, the spell will still work."

Basil shook his head. "The spell must have the exact ingredients for it to work. You know that, as well as I."

"Then we must find a vampire."

"I think I know one west of here," Basil said, looking at his aunt.

"You do?" Sage asked, straightening from his defeated slouch.

A small smile lifted the corners of Mrs. Prescott's mouth. "Perhaps he won't be such trouble, after all. In fact, Melora is the luckiest of your sisters, have I ever told you? The most cunning witch, too. And a brilliant student. Unlike you boys, she paid attention to her lessons."

If you enjoyed *The Witch's Thief*, you'll want to try Tricia Schneider's other books...

THE WITCH AND THE WOLF

Lord Jeremy North's curse is to become a werewolf during every full moon, turning into a bloodthirsty monster that kills with no remorse. When he finds a woman nearly frozen upon his doorstep, his sense of honor compels him to help her, even at the risk he might kill her himself.

Lillian Merriweather hadn't planned to get caught in a blizzard while traveling the English countryside. Nor had she planned on finding refuge in a house full of secrets. But Lillian has secrets of her own. And what she's running from is not far behind...

An excerpt:

There were several moments Jeremy North suspected he suffered hallucinations. Most of those times had been when he had first begun to change into the beast during the full moon. And now, as he answered the knocking he had at first imagined to be the pounding in his skull, he wondered if the brandy he had been drinking this evening was perhaps tainted. He could not quite believe his eyes.

A woman stood on his doorstep, covered in a layer of snow, her bright blue eyes silently pleading to him just before her eyelids fluttered closed, and she crumpled at his feet. He managed to set the candle down safely on a table in time to catch her before she cracked her head on the stone beneath her. He lifted her effortlessly into his arms, brought her into the house, slamming the door closed with his foot. He hurried into the library with his unexpected guest. North had returned earlier seeking the warm oblivion of yet another glass of brandy. He grimaced at the memory of countless other sleep-deprived nights spent in much the same way. *Sans* an unconscious woman, however.

He placed the bundled woman onto the sofa, ignoring the fact that the snow was bound to create a water stain on the fabric once it melted. He leaned over her, pushing the curly brown strands of wet hair off her face and checked to see if she still breathed. Satisfied when he felt her breath on his hand, he went back to the corridor.

"Amery!" He roared.

Turning back to the woman on his sofa, he again felt the necessity to blink his eyes, wondering if they played a trick with his senses. He lit more candles to brighten the room and added more wood to the fire. Then he walked back to the woman and knelt at her side. He found her hand dangling over the edge of the sofa and took it gently in his, the digits frozen stiff. He inhaled a gasp. He cupped both of his hands instinctively around hers, hoping to lend her his warmth.

He heard the shuffle from the hallway and Amery's muttering, then a noisy yawn.

"Bloody hell! What is this?" Amery bellowed from the doorway.

North ignored the query. "We need blankets," he said, instead. "She's frozen through."

Amery nodded and left.

A muffled groan from behind drew his attention, and he turned to see the woman's eyelids flutter open.

He inhaled sharply as her bright blue gaze fell upon him.

She studied him for a moment.

And then, she smiled.

THE WITCH AND THE VAMPIRE

Melora Merriweather is searching for a fellow witch to protect her from a scheming uncle with plans of marriage. When her carriage overturns on her journey, she is rescued by a mysterious man whom she learns is the very person she seeks. But, he's not the witch she thought he was…

Sebastian Collins should have left for London days ago. Now a snowstorm has trapped him with a woman who has come seeking protection, a woman who intrigues him like no other. And with each passing hour, his hunger for her grows…hunger for her kiss, her caress, and her blood.

An excerpt:

"You are Sebastian Collins? Of Caldwell House?" she asked. Had she made some horrible mistake? Who knew how old this letter might be? There had been no date written on any of them. Could this have come from a previous owner of the single address she had managed to discover leading her here? But, no, it could not be possible. Her dreams never misled her.

"Indeed, I am," he answered, relieving her fears. He paused briefly, and then continued, "But there is no Mrs. Collins."

Comprehension dawned. The blush of embarrassment and dread crept up her neck. To her surprise, Mr. Collins stiffened in agitation.

"I-I am truly sorry," she stated, suddenly understanding his reaction. At least, now it made sense why Mrs. Collins never entered her dreams. "I had not realized she had passed. I apologize for the grief I have surely inflicted on you."

"No, no," he said, with a shake of his head. He appeared to have difficulty speaking for a moment until at last, with a deep breath, he reclaimed his composure. Still, he kept his eyes cast down, toward the fire. "You fail to understand. I have never married."

Melora stared at him. Confused, she looked again at the letter in her hand. "But the letters…?"

This time, his head snapped up, and he looked in her direction. She inhaled sharply at the sight of his light blue eyes staring at her. Into her. Through her. Sharp. Piercing. As if he searched her soul for the answers to his questions.

A word about the author...

Tricia Schneider is a paranormal and gothic romance author. Before the supernatural took possession of her pen, she worked for several years in a bookstore as Assistant Manager and bookseller.

Now she writes full-time while raising her three young children. She lives with her musician husband and two neurotic cats in the coal country of Pennsylvania.